Half Baked

A JULI BUTLER MYSTERY
BOOK THREE

BARBARA WITEK

For those whose stories haven't gone as expected.
It's time to turn the page.
B

One

The smell of fresh-brewed coffee and warm cinnamon filled the air as I stacked the last of my signature "B" containers onto the counter, double-checking that the labels were straight. When I started my business, I'd decided to brand the cursive "B" for my last name of Butler, in The Butler's Pantry, where I sold all my organic baked goodies. The pantry side of my business blended nicely into Petite Four Paws Café where people could bring their pets and enjoy organic coffee beverages and light menu options. For the festival, I'd chosen Peanut Butter & Banana Bones for the dogs and Tuna-Nip Kitty Krackers for the cats. My ever-popular roasted pumpkin seeds, for human consumption, filled individual cellophane bags I'd tied with festive fall ribbons were stacked neatly in a couple boxes. If the sales from the Lewis County Fair were any inclination, I was anticipating the Fall Festival to be my busiest weekend yet. I was learning very quickly that New Hope's pets were just as spoiled as their owners.

The harmonious, earthy tone of my wooden chimes sounded as someone came through the door. Without looking up, I called, "If you're here for coffee, I'm running on festival hours—only takeout today."

"I'd be a fool to come between a woman and her festival prep," Chase Hargrave's familiar voice drawled.

I glanced up as he stepped inside, the morning sunlight catching in his dark brown hair. He was dressed in his usual sheriff's department jacket, and a hint of five o'clock shadow lingered on his jaw, like he hadn't quite decided if he was growing it out or just didn't have time to shave. The look suited him—too well, really, but I wasn't letting my thoughts wander down that path.

"Coffee?" I asked, already reaching for a to-go cup.

"Wouldn't say no." He leaned against the counter, watching as I filled it, a devilish twinkle in his green eyes. "You ready for the madness?"

"Almost." I slid the cup toward him. "Just finishing up my festival stash before heading over."

His gaze drifted to the rows of neatly packed treats. "Didn't take you for an exclusive pet bakery."

I smiled. "Then you haven't been paying attention. They are unique and the bulk of my business."

"Guilty as charged." His eyes warmed with amusement. "Major's going to be all over those peanut butter bones."

"I made extra, just in case he and Scallywag decide to stage a coup."

Chase chuckled, taking a sip of coffee. "Probably a smart move."

For a second, things felt almost normal—comfortable, easy. But that illusion shattered the moment the door opened again, and Deputy Gary Maxwell stepped inside. Clean shaven, sandy brown hair all in place, and amber eyes glowing like liquid gold. These men were distinct, yet complementary. Worked great for their line of work. Not so much for my personal life.

Gary hesitated when he saw Chase, a flicker of something unreadable passing across his face before his expression smoothed. "Morning, Juli."

"Morning, Gary." I busied myself by stacking the last of my

containers, ignoring the sudden tension that filled the room. Ever since Chase and I took a relationship "intermission," which had become public knowledge, Gary had been dropping subtle hints of interest. I could handle him on my own but having Chase in the same room complicated things.

"Didn't know you were working festival hours already," Gary said, stepping toward the counter. "Figured I'd stop by before heading over to help with setup."

I smiled, grateful for his attempt at small talk. "Yeah, just wrapping things up here before heading over myself."

Chase cleared his throat, pushing off the counter. "I was just offering to help Juli haul her stuff over."

Gary glanced at him, then at me. "I can help, too."

I suppressed a groan. The last thing I needed this morning was an awkward display of testosterone. "That's sweet of both of you, really, but I've got it covered."

"You sure?" Chase asked, his eyes flicking toward the stacked crates. "Doesn't look like light lifting to me."

"I'm sure," I said, forcing a bright smile. "I need to swing by the *Sunflower Inn* first, check in on Misty before her big event later and drop off some goodies for her gift shop."

Gary nodded. "Right. She's got that amateur bake-off this afternoon."

"And she's already stressed," I added. "Which is why I should probably get over there before she drives herself crazy."

Chase studied me for a beat longer, like he wasn't quite convinced. "Alright. But if you change your mind—"

"I won't." I lifted my coffee in a mock toast. "Go enjoy the festival."

He exhaled, half-amused, half-exasperated, then tipped his cup at me before heading for the door. "You're going to need something other than that sweater. Temps are supposed to drop later this afternoon."

"Thanks, I'll grab my coat from the office."

"See you around, Scarlett."

I watched Chase leave, something heavy settling in my chest.

Gary cleared his throat. "You two—uh, you good?"

I turned back to him, schooling my features into something neutral. "We're...fine."

The way his brows arched in my direction said he wasn't entirely convinced, but he didn't press. Instead, he nodded at the treats. "I think I'll grab a container of those Kitty Krackers before I go. My neighbor's cat keeps glaring at me like I owe it something."

I laughed, handing him a bag, Steve's white paws swatting at my wrist as he jumped up on the counter. "Bribery is the best way to earn a cat's trust. Isn't that right Steve?" I gave his sleek, black fur a long pet from head to tail before gently setting him on the floor. He enjoyed staying at the café. I considered him my guard-cat at keeping the mice away in this old building which had been my mother's antique shop before she died.

"Noted." Gary pulled out his wallet, then paused. "And, uh...if you're free later, maybe we could grab a cider or something?"

I hesitated, caught between gratitude and uncertainty. Gary had been nothing but kind, patient, but with everything that was already on my plate—

"No pressure," he added quickly.

I managed a smile. "I'll see how the day goes."

He nodded, paying for the treats before heading toward the door.

The wooden chimes paused their warm song as Gary stopped at the threshold. "Just so you know, I'm not going to stop asking." He smiled before walking out, and I let out a slow breath.

I headed toward my office and pulled out mom's gray field coat from the closet. I'd found it during the renovations and kept it right where she'd left it. As I put my arms through the sleeves, memories of my mother surrounded me. I straightened the corduroy cuffs and brought the collar close to my nose. The scent of lavender and vanilla grounded me, creating a peaceful moment to my hectic morning.

"How do I handle this, Mom?" I whispered into the quiet. I could almost hear her voice telling me I'd just have to figure it out myself. "Then I'd better get going before the crazy men in my life act like total fools." I stopped to check my reflection in the mirror hanging behind the door, another antique I had to leave in the office. Wearing her coat with my blue eyes and auburn waves draped over my shoulders, I looked like the younger version of her I'd seen in old pictures. I smiled at myself, and it was as if she really was smiling back at me. "Okay," I said and nodded, closing the door on my way out.

It was going to be a long day.

And something told me the festival wasn't the only thing stirring up trouble this weekend.

———

I PULLED MY CHERRY-RED PICKUP TRUCK INTO THE gravel lot of the *Sunflower Inn*, the sight of the large banner hanging from the front porch creating a wide smile on my face. "The Sunflower Inn Presents: The Return of the Amateur Bake-Off."

I hopped out of my seat, the smell of woodsmoke from the festival fire pits mingling with the crisp autumn air, bringing memories of past festivals to mind. Even with the golden sunlight bathing the inn's wraparound porch, it looked...tired. The once cheerful, pristine, white-washed brick was fading, and the railing leading up the steps wobbled slightly under my grip.

Inside, I found Misty Shepard hunched over a large book at the reception desk, chewing on the end of her pen. Her chocolate brown hair had been twisted low on her neck and held in place with a large orange clip, which perfectly matched her cardigan.

"You look like you're plotting something," I said, setting my box of treats for the inn's gift shop onto the counter.

She startled, then relaxed when she saw me. "Juli! You're just in time. I was about to head over to the festival, but I needed a minute to—" She gestured vaguely at the disarray of papers in front of her.

I leaned in, my eyebrows lifted. "I can't believe you're bringing back the high school bake-off!"

Misty gave a small, proud smile. "It was one of my favorite events when my parents ran the inn. We haven't done it in years, but I figured it was time. The kids have been so excited. I've been getting updates all morning."

"That's amazing, Misty." I meant it. The festival was filled with competitions—best pie, best preserves, sack races—but this had always been a chance for younger bakers to shine.

"I just hope I don't regret it," she said, organizing the last of the forms. "So far, everything that can go wrong has gone wrong for this weekend."

Before I could ask what she meant, the front door swung open, banging against the wall with unnecessary force.

"Ladies, what a sight," came a voice laced with syrupy condescension. Liza Blake strode in like she owned the place, a sleek burgundy coat cinched at her waist, her blonde hair styled to perfection. "Misty, I thought I'd stop in before heading to the festival, but I see you're...busy."

Misty stiffened. "Liza."

I folded my arms, staying silent but keeping my eyes on Liza. I vaguely remembered her from school. We ran in separate circles, and as I watched the drama unfolding before me, I started to recall why.

Liza scanned the room, filler-enhanced lips curling in distaste. "Charming...in that inherited clutter sort of way. I suppose when you come from old New Hope stock, you don't have to worry about appearances." Her eyes locked on mine. "Your father certainly didn't—not with the company he kept. Everyone knew Jackson Butler had...connections."

"Let me guess," I said dryly holding nothing back, "mob ties or secret treasure maps?" I'd heard all kinds of rumors after my dad left town. Didn't believe a single one of them. He'd made an honest living as a mechanic, loved his family and friends. Mom always told me he had an itch for adventure and that's where I got it from.

"Oh, I wouldn't dare assume," Liza's voice interrupted my thoughts. "But secrets have a way of sticking to a name, don't they?" Liza circled the room, coming to stand directly in front of Misty. "It's a shame, really. This place used to be the pride of New Hope, and now..." She let out a dramatic sigh. "I suppose I should thank you. Due to all your canceled reservations, I'm completely booked at my bed-and-breakfast. You were aware I recently bought out the old Lyndon place, right? Guests who were supposed to stay here, well, I guess they decided they'd rather not deal with such a dilapidated inn."

Misty's hands curled into fists. "We had to cancel because of—"

"Oh, I know. Water problems. Electrical problems. Faulty heating." Liza ticked off each item on her fingers. "So many unfortunate incidents. I'd almost think someone was trying to drive you out of business."

And there was Liza, stirring the pot as usual.

Misty's face flushed, but before she could respond, Liza clapped her hands together. "Well, must be off! My guests expect a superior experience." With that, she turned on the heel of her fancy leather boot and swept out the door, leaving us in a stunned silence.

I let loose a whoosh of breath. "Want to tell me what *that* was about?"

Misty sagged into the nearest chair as if Liza's appearance had sucked the life out of her. "It's true. We've had one thing after another go wrong these past few months. First, pipes burst in two of the rooms. Then, the electrical system shorted out in the dining room. Last week, when that storm blew through, a window mysteriously shattered in one of our best suites."

My stomach twisted. "You think someone's sabotaging you?"

She rubbed her forehead, then raked her unpolished nails through her hair. "Why sabotage me? I think it's just bad luck. But we've had to cancel so many reservations we're barely at half capacity this weekend."

I frowned. "And Oliver's been helping?"

My best friend had relocated from Boston and had plans to stay with me until he figured out his next move. I, of course, was thrilled that he'd decided to turn his catering business, *Savory Elegance*, into a restaurant right here in New Hope. He'd been working with a real estate agent to find the perfect spot.

She nodded. "Oliver has been great. But there's only so much he can do. We need major repairs, and I don't have the money or the crew to do them all at once."

Before I could respond, the front door opened again, and April Henderson strolled in, flipping her blonde hair over one shoulder. "Was that Liza Blake? Is she in town for the festival? Oh my gosh, we should all catch up. It would be like old times!"

I refrained from groaning out loud. April loved to fan the flames, preferably while looking oblivious, as if she couldn't already see the distress on Misty's face.

"Why are you here?" I had to ask.

"I saw your truck outside. I hope you don't mind—I had to call Chase for a little plumbing issue," she said breezily. "He's such a gentleman. Came right over. I thanked him properly, of course, with a home cooked meal. That man just loves my meatloaf." She giggled. "And my cherry tarts."

I bit the inside of my cheek, willing myself not to react. I had no right to be irritated, after all, Chase and I were taking a relationship intermission. But somehow, knowing Chase had dropped everything to help my nemesis, when he and I had barely been able to say more than a few words to each other, rubbed me the wrong way. I wouldn't put it past her to be taking full advantage of our situation. April had always been waiting for any opportunity to have Chase to herself.

Misty shot me a knowing look, but I ignored it. As much as I wanted to call April out, I decided to channel my mother and take the higher road.

"Festival's calling," I said, tapping my knuckles against the check-in counter on my way out the door. "See you at the bake-off, Misty."

Two

By the time I crossed Miller Park and reached the festival's baking tent, the amateur competition was already in full swing. Tables were set up with rows of pies, cakes, and cookies, their sugary aromas congregating amid the brisk fall breeze. Pumpkins, carved into goofy grins and painted on scenes, lined the tent's entrance. Bales of hay served as seating for those lingering to watch the competition unfold. Nearby, children squealed as they played pumpkin tic-tac-toe on a giant grid spray painted on the ground, others maneuvered carefully balancing colorful fall leaves on spoons in the autumn leaf race. Their laughter cutting through the cool air.

Beside me, Betty Henderson—April's aunt and longtime festival judge—sighed as she sipped mulled cider from a plastic cup. A light breeze fluffed her blonde curly hair. "It's so nice to see this tradition back," she said in her sweet southern accent. The woman swore by southern roots somewhere in her bloodline, while she'd never been outside of the state of Connecticut. "Remember when y'all used to participate back when Pam and Stew Shepard ran it?"

"I think Misty's hoping to make it a permanent event again," I said, releasing a contented sigh of my own over yet another fall memory, and gave my friend a thumbs-up a she set up the contestants and their entries.

Betty chuckled softly. "You four girls would be so fired up every single year. Misty, you, April...and Liza." Her voice dropped. "That Liza, she was something else."

"Yeah," I muttered, "something else all right." I contemplated my next statement then decided to go for it. "Speaking of something else, what's April been up to? I hear she had plumbing problems." Not that I didn't believe April, but I adored her aunt, and Betty was well known for her ability to gossip. If anyone would be straight with me, it was Betty Henderson. I just needed to know if April was purposely stirring the pot.

Betty smiled, ready to respond, when Liza materialized in a light blue cowl neck sweater beneath a navy down vest, acid washed designer jeans, and a pair of work boots with a thick, chunky heal, making me wonder why she needed a wardrobe change, who she was trying to impress...or intimidate. She walked with an air of confidence, chin high, shoulders squared.

Her voice was sharp and cutting as she clapped her hands to accentuate each word when she spoke, "Well, well. The *Sunflower Inn*, back in the game." She paused and glanced around, making sure those of us close enough were paying attention. Her smile stretched tight, more smug than friendly, "A bold move, Misty."

Misty stiffened behind the judging table, forcing a smile. I didn't miss the strain in her voice or her fingers twitching at her sides, as the breeze kicked up around us. "I see you haven't changed a bit, Liza."

Liza puckered her lips, making them look twice their inflated size, as she surveyed the baked goods. "Funny, I seem to remember winning this competition *every* year. Even though your parents ran it, isn't that funny? Must be they didn't have any faith in you, either."

Betty let out a disapproving grunt. "Now, now, Liza dear, that was a long time ago."

Liza ignored Betty, turning her attention back to Misty. "I do hope you're setting these kids up for real competition. No use filling their heads with false confidence if they can't actually bake."

Misty's jaw clenched. "That's not what this is about. It's about encouraging them."

Liza's eyes flashed with a glint of both amusement and superiority. "Of course. Encouragement is all some people have left. You would know that firsthand, wouldn't you?"

Misty's face burned with frustration, her fingers curling into fists. I braced myself when Misty's words dripped with venom, "And what about you? Don't think we never heard the rumors about how you really won every year."

"Oooo..." the gathering crowd moaned.

"Even after all these years, you're still jealous." Liza took a step closer.

"Of your cheating? Never." Misty crossed her arms. "I had better self-esteem and didn't need to perform favors to win anything."

"Rumors. Probably started by you and your so-called friends." Liza's eyes cut to me.

I was about to let her know how I really felt about her when I noticed Misty's usually smiling face morph into something almost menacing. "Tell me, Liza, did you use the same technique to get your hands on the Lyndon place?" The crowd gasped, and Misty continued, "I'm only wondering because when it was on the market, they were asking far more than what it was worth."

"How I do my business is none of yours. Why don't you stop talking before you look like more of a fool than you already are for hanging on to the town eyesore." Liza extended an arm in the direction of the inn.

Misty's face flushed bright red. "Don't you talk about the *Sunflower Inn* like that! My family has owned the inn for generations. I promised my parents I would continue their legacy, and I will restore the inn to its original glory."

"Well, you're not doing a very good job. The place is falling apart around you. You don't know how to run a business, you never could get a man, and you won the pie contest at the fair most likely out of pity. I heard the second-place winner had a better tasting pie than yours." Liza leaned across the judging table, nose to nose with Misty. "Bribe a judge much? I've also heard the main judge was a little smitten with you. Is that true?"

"Shut your mouth, Liza!" Misty yelled, slamming her palms on the table, and I swear I heard thunder rumble in the distance.

I glanced around anxiously, noticing how silent the crowd had grown, and how dark the sky was becoming. No one was stepping in. Where was Chase? Gary? Young deputy Liam? I felt as if this could escalate at any moment.

I watched in horror as Misty's edge collapsed at the mention of Oliver, who had judged the contest. I caught the subtle quiver of her chin as she quickly scanned the crowd. Thankfully, Ollie wasn't here because he would have inserted himself to defend her. This scene didn't need to get any bigger than it already was.

"Oops, did I hit a nerve? Must be the rumors are true then." Liza harrumphed and pushed herself away from the table. "Don't play the game unless you intend to win. But seriously, you should think about selling the place. Save your parents the embarrassment."

"You're the only one playing games, Liza. And I'll beat you at your own game, just wait."

"Please." Liza fanned her face dramatically. "I'll even do you a favor and make a more than fair offer."

"I would never sell to the likes of you!" Misty rounded the table, hands fisted at her sides. "Maybe you're the one who's been sabotaging me on purpose to force me out. Maybe you're afraid of honest competition!"

"Me? Afraid of you?" Liza let loose a wicked laugh that made me scan the sky for flying monkeys.

"Maybe you should be." There was more than an edge to Misty's voice this time and the autumn breeze seemed to still in the trees.

I zipped my jacket around my neck to keep out the sudden chill when Misty and Liza exchanged a fierce glare. There wasn't even a murmur from the crowd as we all waited to see what would happen next.

"We'll see who's the real winner at the end of the festival. I've gotten amazing feedback at my bed and breakfast. My guests are already reserving a year in advance!"

"Don't count your poppies before they put you to sleep, Liza. The festival has just begun, and I can assure *you* won't be winning anything."

Liza narrowed her eyes at Misty and without saying another word stormed away, leaving a wake of tension and a trail of swirling leaves behind her.

"Whew!" Betty huffed, breaking the awkward silence. "That girl always did know how to push buttons."

I just nodded, my eyes following Liza as she disappeared into the crowd. An icy chill crept down my spine, leaving me unsettled by an impending dread I couldn't shake off.

AFTER THE BAKE-OFF ENDED, OLIVER AND I WANDERED toward the back of the tent. "Wow, what a fun event. It brought back all the memories," I said with a giant smile on my face. "Who would have thought it would come down to a pair of ten-year-old twins?"

"Spectacular display of talent and creativity. Betty did a wonderful job being the tie breaking judge." Oliver remarked, then stopped short at the sight of Misty pacing.

"She's infuriating," Misty muttered as she dropped into the nearest chair. "I could barely finish the bake-off."

Oliver crouched in front of her, his lean frame folding easily into the small space. His blond hair was slightly tousled like he'd rushed over without a second thought. "Hey," he said softly, placing a calming hand on her knee, his blue eyes searching her face. "She's trying to get under your skin. Ignore her."

Misty shook her head as if trying to keep her tears at bay. "It's not that easy. You don't know her. She's always been an awful person."

"That wicked witch of a woman isn't worth your energy," Oliver added, a small grin playing on his lips. "You know, I can think of a great way to lift your spirits. What about dinner tonight? I'll do the cooking and the cleanup."

Misty shook her head but didn't push him away. Instead, she smiled and relaxed into him. "Thanks, Oliver. How can I say no to that?"

Oliver pulled her in fully for a hug. I heard Misty sigh and Oliver hugged her tighter, giving me a wink from over her shoulder. Since judging the pie contest at the fair, Oliver had been trying to get to know Misty better. I smiled and spotted Claire Bennett lingering at the edge of the festival grounds. Her gaze was locked on them. Though her face was mostly still, the slight clench of her jaw gave away her discomfort. I saw her swipe across her eyes, then she turned abruptly and slipped down a wooded path. I knew it had been a close finish between her pie and Misty's at the County Fair. I wasn't sure why she was so visibly upset but felt almost compelled to talk to her.

"Hey, if you guys will excuse me, I just saw someone I've been waiting to connect with."

Oliver's eyes sparkled with amusement. "Would that be the good sheriff...or his loyal deputy?"

I tossed my hands in the air with an overexaggerated grunt and hurried away to the sounds of both Oliver and Misty laughing.

Under normal circumstances I'd play along, but my worry meter hummed low in my gut, and I wasn't about to ignore it. Chase and Gary would have to wait.

"Claire, hold up!" I called when I caught sight of her honey brown ponytail at the first bend on the trail. She stopped but didn't turn around. "You okay?" I asked gently when I reached her.

She let out a short burst of laughter, shaking her head. "I see the way Oliver looks at her. I can't get him to even notice me, especially when Misty's around. He will never look at me that way."

I frowned. "Claire—"

"It doesn't matter." She finally faced me, her brown eyes hard and glassy from tears. "I don't stand a chance against her. Second to her at the fair and not even in the running with Oliver."

"Oh Claire, I don't think Oliver has a clue about how you feel. He's one of my best friends and the nicest man I know. He would never set out to hurt you or your feelings, and he'd feel terrible if he knew you felt this way."

"I've tried to talk to him, Juli. He doesn't even see me. Oliver is so in love with Misty and she's too preoccupied with the inn to notice or even care," her voice hitched, and she turned away for a moment, composing herself. "You know," she added softly, "It's not just about Oliver. Misty...she always gets what she wants. She doesn't even try, and luck just falls into her lap. Meanwhile, I work just as hard, if not harder, but I never seem to measure up." She shook her head, her breath shaky as she fought more tears. "And now Oliver, too? No matter what I do, I'll never be enough."

I swallowed hard, understanding more than I wanted to admit. "Oliver isn't the kind of guy to fall for someone just because they are lucky or charming. He's loyal, thoughtful...and stubborn." I smiled, hoping to send some positive vibes her way. "If Misty isn't what he really wants, he'll figure it out."

Claire sniffed, her smile weak. "I guess I'll just have to wait and see."

Suddenly I wondered if there was any truth to what Claire was saying. Ever since the fair, Oliver had been spending a lot of time getting to know Misty. We'd all cooked together, and he'd been helping her with repairs around the inn. Yet he'd never confided in me that they'd been romantic or so much as even kissed each other. Was the relationship one-sided? Was Oliver too blind to see it?

I nodded, unsure of what else to say. As Claire turned to leave, I couldn't get rid of the tension winding through my body. Something about her bitterness lingered like a thick mist after the rain. And I couldn't shake the feeling that her frustration might lead her toward something drastic.

Three

The next day, the Fall Festival was in full swing, the air heavy with the scent of roasted nuts, caramel apples, and fried dough. Bright orange and red banners fluttered from the vendor booths within *Miller Park*, and kids darted between game stalls, their laughter carrying over the live music playing from the gazebo.

I took a moment to soak it all in.

The funnel cake stand already had a line wrapped around the corner, a local farm had set up a make-your-own caramel apple station, and the hiking trails leading through the park were crowded with festivalgoers taking in the autumn foliage. Near the main path, a friendly pumpkin bowling competition was underway as kids rolled small pumpkins toward stacked hay bales setup behind plastic bottles painted like bowling pins.

I made my way toward my "Barking for Apples" booth, where I had set up a large kiddie pool of water filled with floating apples. The twist? The apples had my home-made treats tied to the stems, and dogs had to bob for them while their owners cheered them on.

I was adjusting the water level when I heard the familiar jangle of a leash, followed by a deep, eager *Woof-Woof!* I glanced up to see

Chase approaching my booth with Major. The big lug of a sheepdog was barely able to control himself. He didn't know whether to wiggle with happiness or yank his master down the path.

"Well, if it isn't my favorite troublemaker," I said, smiling as I patted his shaggy mop of a head.

"You talking about him or me?" Chase teased, pointing between himself and the dog as they came to a stop.

"You? Trouble?" I said, feeling mischievous. Then shaking my head, I added in a teasing tone, "Never."

Major stomped his large furry feet furiously, eyes locked on the apple pool like he'd just found buried treasure. "Let's see if he's got what it takes," Chase said, crouching down to unclip the leash.

As soon as Major felt the freedom, he lunged—straight into the pool.

Water splashed everywhere. I let out a yelp, dodging the worst of it as Chase groaned. "Major, no..." But it was too late. He pounced and continuously dunked his head, creating a series of waves in the pool as more water and apples sloshed over the sides. He finally emerged, completely soaked, an apple clenched between his teeth. Looking incredibly proud of himself, he jumped out of the pool and gave his sopping waves of fur a giant shake. A shower of water followed, hitting everyone in the immediate area.

I wiped droplets off my arms, clapping my hands with excitement when he dropped the apple at my feet. "You got one. Good boy!"

Chase sighed. "He's determined, I'll give him that."

"Just like his owner," I said and handed him a towel to dry off.

"You ought to know." He cast a devilish grin, instantly creating the comfortable energy that was *us*. I knew why he was giving me space, but that didn't mean I had to like it. I wanted things the way they used to be, but every time I felt like I could move forward I was reminded why I kept stepping back. Since I'd returned home, he'd made it pretty clear he wanted answers as to why I left. His giving me time and space to figure things out only made me more frustrated.

Nearby, a whistle blew, signaling the start of the sack race. Chase re-leashed Major and we turned to see Mark Walker, my café manager, lining up with his wife and two daughters. They each stepped into burlap sacks, gripping the edges as they prepared to hop toward the finish line.

"Mark's got some stiff competition," I said, nudging Chase.

"I don't know," Chase said while pointing toward Mark's children. "Those girls look like they mean business."

"I'm so glad Cindy and Mark worked things out and are back together, stronger than ever." I knew the double meaning in my words. I didn't intend for them to come out that way and I could tell Chase picked up on it, too.

"He was a huge help in the first case we worked on. I'm glad Cindy understood the importance of why we couldn't tell her anything until it was over, and he could finally fill her in on all the details."

I pursed my lips in thought, wondering if there was a double meaning to what Chase was saying, too. I had my reasons for leaving back then, and a whole lot of explaining to do. But I still wasn't sure if I could go down that road again. Hence our continued dilemma.

We cheered as the race kicked off. Mark's youngest tripped two hops in, landing with a giggle before scrambling to her feet. The crowd roared with encouragement, and we found ourselves cheering along with them, basking in the carefree energy.

Just what Chase and I needed.

But my light mood flickered when I spotted Misty across the park, talking to someone I didn't recognize. He was tall, broad-shouldered, wearing a denim jacket and an easy smile as he leaned in slightly, listening to Misty. There was something familiar about him, but I couldn't place it.

"Who's that?" I asked, tilting my head.

Chase followed my gaze. "That's Ethan Harris."

I blinked. "Ethan? As in...the guy who was a year ahead of us in school?" I did a double take as Chase confirmed with a nod. "I remember him being shy and nerdy. He's all buff and handsome now."

"He's been helping Misty at the inn on and off for a while." Chase gave me a knowing look. "He's always had a thing for her. Can't seem to let her go."

Again, with the double entendres!

A small frown pulled at my lips as I ignored Chase's little slip. "I wonder if she's mentioned him to Oliver?" The last thing I wanted was for my best friend to get hurt.

Chase shook his head, clearly amused. "Juli, you're over-reacting."

I crossed my arms. "Well, maybe someone shouldn't give me a reason to."

His brows lifted. "Oh?"

I turned, meeting his gaze. "April. Plumbing. Ringing any bells, Lawman?"

Chase's mouth twitched like he was fighting a smile. "Are you...jealous?"

I hesitated—then sighed as I honestly responded, "Maybe a little."

He chuckled. "There's an easy resolution, you know."

Oh, I knew.

I had played the scenarios out in my head for weeks since our intermission—I refused to call it a break—and couldn't figure out which option had the better outcome. Tell him the truth of what drove my decision to leave New Hope and hope we'd be able to move forward or tell him a half-truth and risk staying the way we were. Chase stared, his head cocked as if waiting for my response. The one I couldn't formulate. Before I could deflect, Major caught sight of Harry Henderson and took off, dragging Chase with him.

"Saved by the cookie," I muttered because Harry always carried treats in his hardware apron pockets, and he was rarely without his apron. "Guess we're done here," I called, watching as Chase stumbled after his dog.

Which was far better than watching me stumble over my words.

———

MISTY'S PASTRY BOOTH STOOD NEAR THE CENTER OF the festival, framed in the late afternoon light by twinkling fairy lights strung along the awning. A chalkboard menu, written in elegant cursive, listed her seasonal treats: spiced apple tarts, pumpkin cream puffs, maple pecan scones, and cinnamon-glazed donuts. A small wicker basket of mini pie samples sat invitingly at the edge of the counter, and a few pumpkins with delicate hand-painted designs decorated the display.

As I made my way through the bustling festival, a vibrant mix of gold, russet, and burnt orange leaves rustled gently in the October breeze. The chatter of festivalgoers hummed around me, and I could hear the next band warming up on the entertainment stage at the gazebo.

Misty stood behind the table arranging trays of spiced apple tarts with careful precision, her brow slightly furrowed in concentration. She looked up as I approached, brushing a few stray strands of hair from her face with the back of her hand.

"So," I said, plucking a tart from the sample tray and taking a bite. Flaky crust, sweet apples, just the right amount of spice. "I see Ethan's back in town."

Misty let out a slow sigh, her hands stilling for a moment before she picked up a cloth and began absently wiping her fingers. "I figured you'd ask," she said quietly.

I raised an eyebrow. "And?"

She glanced at me, then back down at the tray, rearranging pastries that didn't need rearranging. "C'mon, we all grew up together," she said finally. "We dated once long after you left town. He even proposed a few years back, but I wasn't ready for that kind of commitment."

I studied her carefully, trying to gauge what she wasn't saying. "What about now?"

Her fingers tightened around the cloth. "Ethan still comes around. But I don't see him that way. We're just friends."

I sagged slightly, my tension easing. Good. That meant there was still a chance Oliver wouldn't get his heart broken. "And Oliver?" I asked, trying to keep my tone light. "How do you see him?"

Misty hesitated. A strand of mocha brown hair fell loose from her pink clip, and she swiped it away, her expression briefly uncertain. "I like him," she admitted. "A lot." Then she bit her lip.

"But?" I prompted.

She sighed. "But sometimes he's...too much."

I nodded slowly, understanding more than I wanted to admit. Oliver had a way of throwing himself into things—projects, relationships, ideas—wholeheartedly, without hesitation. It was part of what made him charming, but I could see how it might be overwhelming, too.

"Too much, how?" I asked carefully.

Misty exhaled through her nose, setting down the cloth and folding her arms. "He's so intense, and sometimes...I feel like I can't breathe."

That surprised me. Misty had always been independent, but I'd never known her to feel smothered by someone's attention. "Does he know you feel that way?" I asked.

She hesitated again. "Not really."

"And do you...plan to tell him? He would want to know." Just then, Gary walked up, hands in his pockets, wearing his usual easy smile and conveniently cutting off Misty's response.

"Hi, Juli," he said smoothly. "Festival's looking great this year."

Misty's gaze flicked to me, mischief flashing in her brown eyes. I ignored it.

Gary leaned casually against the booth, his jacket unzipped just enough to show his badge clipped to his belt. The way he carried himself made me wonder if he was like Chase and always on duty.

"My shift just ended, and I was hoping to catch you," he said, his voice light, but there was an undercurrent of something else. "Maybe for that cider we talked about?"

I hesitated—again.

Misty, of course, seized the moment. "Oh, don't let me stop you," she said, arching a brow as she rearranged a tray of maple pecan scones.

I shot her with a warning glare, which she conveniently ignored.

"Busy?" Gary asked, watching me carefully.

"Just...a lot on my mind," I admitted, rubbing my fingers over the worn fabric of mom's jacket sleeve.

Misty leaned on the table, tapping her nails on the hard surface. "A cider might help with that," she mused.

"Or whiskey," I muttered under my breath.

Gary grinned. "I know a place that has both."

Misty snorted.

I sighed, rolling my eyes. "I'll think about it."

Gary looked like he wanted to say something else, but before he could, his cell phone beeped, and he pulled it from his jacket pocket. He frowned, glancing down as he read a text message.

"Looks like duty calls," he said, sighing dramatically. "Gotta help Liam at the station."

Misty smiled knowingly. "Poor timing, Deputy Maxwell."

Gary flashed her a grin, then turned his attention back to me. "I'll check in later." Then he was gone, disappearing into the crowd, leaving behind the scent of coffee and cedarwood.

Misty pointed a finger at me. "You know," she said, dragging out the words, "Gary is very nice."

I narrowed my eyes. "Don't start."

She chuckled, lifting a delicate sugar-dusted tart and taking a bite. "Just saying."

"Noted."

She chewed thoughtfully. "So, about Oliver..."

I stiffened slightly. "What about him?"

Misty's eyes softened with understanding. "You're worried about him."

I sighed. "I just don't want to see him get hurt."

Misty nodded slowly. "Neither do I. Now if you want to help me for real, I have plenty for you to do." She handed me a box of pastries, pointing to an empty shelf in her display case, and went to fetch more.

Her words regarding Ollie should have reassured me. But something about the way she said it didn't. She wasn't saying she wouldn't hurt him. She was saying she didn't want to.

And that was a very different thing.

I forced a smile as I got to work, but my chest felt tight. Oliver was an all-in kind of guy, always had been. And if Misty wasn't ready to be...

Maybe Oliver's heart was on the line after all. I shivered as I buttoned up mom's field coat already worrying that trouble might be brewing.

Four

"Come on, Juli," Gary said an hour later, flashing his best smile. Laughter and the occasional cheer from a game booth echoed over the park, blending with the upbeat music of a folk band playing near the gazebo. "It's just dinner. Or that cider, if you prefer." He grinned teasingly. "Maybe a few games at the festival. We're friends, right?" He fiddled with his watch band and rocked back on his heels in front of Misty and me.

"I know," I said slowly, still unsure. "It's just been...busy." I sounded lame repeating the same thing yet again, but I truly didn't know what else to say.

"Exactly! You need a break." His voice softened and he gave me that earnest look that was hard to argue with. "I'm not asking you to run away with me or anything. Just take some time and unwind." He gave me a puppy dog look. "A guy can only take crashing and burning so many times. Have mercy on me. What do you say?"

I hesitated, but before I could find another excuse, Misty nudged me with her elbow. "Go. Have some fun," she encouraged. "You've done enough here. I'll be fine, and Gary's right, you deserve it." She smiled sweetly at Gary, and I wondered if they were in cahoots. "It's nice to see someone making an effort."

That caught me off guard. Misty wasn't usually one to offer romantic advice. And her tone...did I detect a hint of smugness?

"Fine," I said with a sigh, watching colorful leaves of burnt orange and deep gold twirl through the air before settling onto the stone paths winding between booths, distracting me from Gary's casual invitation. "Cider sounds good, and maybe a couple games."

Gary beamed and fist pumped into the air. "Yes! You made my day, Juli Butler." He checked his phone and groaned over another text. "Listen, I'll find you later." He pointed a finger at me. "You're not getting off the hook this time. You said yes, and I have witnesses."

"Okay!" I laughed and gave him a playful shove away from the booth. "Go!"

Gary spun around and ran into poor Sally Sweet, almost knocking her over. "Excuse me, Sally!" He steadied her, his smile wide.

"Oh, dear!" she exclaimed as she relied on his biceps to regain her balance.

"I'm so sorry, are you okay?" he asked.

"That was totally my fault," I jumped in, "I shouldn't have shoved Gary."

"I'm fine." Sally glanced around, a little rattled. "I should have been paying more attention. I got caught up in looking at everyone's wonderful booths when I should have watched where I was going. I'd love to chat, but I need to get back to the shop." Sally waved and continued on her way.

"And I need to get back to work." He pointed his finger at me again and winked.

"I'll be ready, I promise!" I called toward his back as he walked away. I couldn't stop smiling. Gary was fun. Maybe a little fun wouldn't hurt.

Until a sharp, familiar voice cut through the chatter like a well-honed knife.

"Misty, Misty, Misty," Liza purred as she sauntered forward, a satisfied grin curling her extra-large lips. The super glossy burgundy lipstick made them appear to jump off her face. "Still at it with the pastries, huh?"

I turned, watching as Misty's jaw clenched. She didn't respond, but her hands, usually steady and confident while working, trembled slightly as she moved a tray of cherry danish.

Liza's sharp hazel eyes gleamed, as if she had noticed Misty's barely contained frustration and was relishing the reaction.

"Remember that other contest when you were disqualified because your pie was half-baked?" Liza continued, her voice dripping with mock concern.

Misty inhaled sharply. Her lips pressed into a thin line.

I could see another battle waging inside her—the desperate attempt to keep her temper in check. Misty wasn't quick to anger, but Liza had a way of poking at old wounds with surgical precision. She'd always done this, but this seemed worse, intentional. Almost like she had an agenda of some sort.

"I wonder if you'll sabotage yourself again," Liza taunted. "Or maybe you'll continue to blame others when things go wrong. I must say, I think that's about the only thing you're good at."

Misty's eyes narrowed. "I don't know what your problem is, Liza, but it's exhausting."

"My problem?" Liza's smile sharpened as if she were coming in for the kill. "We both know you're in over your head. Just give it up already. You've been nothing but a mess since you took over that rundown inn. Might want to stop chasing impossible dreams before you completely lose them."

"What exactly are you talking about?"

"Oh, wait. If I remember correctly, running the inn was never one of your dreams, now was it? You only took on all this responsibility because your parents retired early and made you feel bad about your choices. You've always been the weak link, Misty." Liza eyed the baked goods like a jealous, evil stepsister and they weren't even related. "You should have stuck up for yourself, followed your own path not the path of your parents."

"I wasn't pushed into taking over the inn. I love what I do." Misty marched over to Liza. "Everyone loves my cooking and baking!"

"I'll be the judge of that." Liza let out a low chuckle, slow and deliberate. "Let's hope you've improved over the years," she mused, reaching for a slice of caramel apple cobbler displayed on Misty's table. Misty opened her mouth—maybe to protest, maybe to finally snap—but Liza ignored her, lifting the dessert and taking a deliberate bite.

I watched as she chewed slowly, making an exaggerated show of smacking her lips.

"I don't care what you think," Misty bit out, her voice strained.

Liza swallowed and licked the sticky caramel from her fingers, dragging out the moment. She met Misty's gaze with a gleam of satisfaction. "Not bad," she mused, ignoring her. "But let's see if it's fully cooked this time."

She took another greedy bite. And another, and another, grabbing two more pieces as if she were purposely trying to ruin all of the slices for everyone else. Then, her expression changed. Her lips twisted, brows furrowing as she cleared her throat. The sinister edge to her expression vanished. A strange wheezing sound escaped her lips. Her eyes widened in alarm.

I took a step forward, suddenly uneasy. "Liza?"

She grabbed at her throat, fingers trembling. A strangled sound escaped her lips, raw and desperate.

My stomach dropped. Something was wrong.

"Liza?" I said again, sharper this time. "Are you choking?"

She let out a guttural gasp, her movements growing frantic. Her hands clutched her throat, then her gaze met mine, panicked and desperate. She stumbled forward, reaching out and grabbing my arm in a vice-like grip. I barely had time to react before her body seized violently.

Gary appeared out of nowhere, rushing forward with wide eyes. "Juli! Someone said there was an emergency here. Are you all right? What happened?" he barked before noticing Liza. "What's wrong with her?" He rushed over in full deputy mode to attend to her distress.

"I–I don't know," I stammered. "She just—"

And then, she collapsed.

The world around us blurred into chaos. Gasps and shrieks echoed through the festival, and someone screamed for help. Misty stood frozen in shock, eyes locked onto Liza's motionless body.

"Call an ambulance!" I yelled, my pulse thundering in my ears.

Gary was already pulling out his radio, calling for emergency services, but I knew. It was too late.

Liza Blake was dead.

———

An hour later, the festive energy of the park had shifted dramatically. The once vibrant stalls and booths now felt muted, swallowed by the flashing lights of police cruisers and the coroner's van.

Liza's lifeless body lay beneath a protective covering near Misty's booth, her once-flushed face now pale and still. The once sweet aroma of caramel apples and baked goods now mixed with something else, something sinister. I stood near the booth, arms wrapped around myself, still trying to make sense of what had happened. Chase stood a few feet away, his expression unreadable as he listened to the coroner.

Conrad Ripton, affectionately known as Rip, New Hope's coroner, finally stepped back from the body, rubbing his face tiredly. "We'll need to confirm with toxicology," he said, his voice low, "but my initial findings are leading me to believe Liza was poisoned."

"You don't say," Chase stroked his fingers along his stubbled jaw.

"Deputy Maxwell confirmed the victim was seizing when he arrived on the scene. There seems to be some irritation around her mouth, apparent drool and signs of foaming toward the back of her throat."

A sharp, cold weight settled in my stomach. My worry meter spiked. This was not a choking incident. Not a freak accident.

Poison. Murder.

Chase's gaze flickered toward me, searching, assessing. His voice was calm and controlled when he spoke. "The pie was Misty's, wasn't it?"

I swallowed hard, my throat tight as I confirmed with a slow nod.

Misty—who stood paralyzed beside Ethan—let out a strangled sob. "That's not possible," she whispered, shaking her head. "I—I made the cobbler myself. I tasted the batter. I—" Her voice broke. Ethan wrapped an arm around her shoulders, pulling her close. She turned, burying her face in his chest, her entire body trembling.

"Hey, hey, I've got you," Ethan murmured, his voice soft but firm. "This isn't your fault."

Misty's fingers fisted into the front of his jacket as she choked on a sob. "What if, what if someone—"

"No," Ethan cut in firmly. "We're not going there. Someone else did this, Misty. Someone who wanted to hurt you. I'm not going to let that happen. I'll call my father and have him send his lawyer." His eyes met Chase's, flashing with protective fire. "I don't want her answering any questions without me or our lawyer there," Ethan ordered. "You got that?"

"I got it," Chase replied cooly, not rising to the bait. "She's going to have to talk to me either way."

"Fine," Ethan growled. "Not tonight."

Misty shivered in his arms, her body clinging to his as though she'd fall apart if he should let go. "I didn't do anything wrong," she whispered. "I would never hurt someone."

"I know, babe," Ethan said softly, his hand stroking her hair. "I know."

Something about the way she clung to him made my stomach twist—not in suspicion, but in realization. She needed him. And he was there. I glanced at Oliver, who had rushed onto the scene the minute he'd heard about the incident. He stood rigidly beside me, his hands clenched into tight fists. His gaze had locked on the duo, but his expression wasn't just concern, it was something more.

Jealousy.

I glanced around the scene. "This doesn't make sense," I said, shaking my head. "Misty would never—"

"She's our number one suspect," Chase interrupted, his voice firm as Sheriff Do-Good returned to action.

I spun around, my anger flaring. "You can't seriously think Misty—"

He lifted a hand, stopping me. "Juli, I don't want to believe it either. But the fact remains—the dessert came from her booth."

I pressed my lips together, frustration bubbling beneath the surface. "She wouldn't do this," I said quietly.

"I know." Chase's voice softened just enough that I felt my chest tighten. He shifted closer, lowering his tone even more. "Look, I'm doing my job right now. But later..." his gaze held mine, steady and intense. "We'll talk. I promise."

I started to protest, but the strain on his face kept me quiet. Chase was holding it together, but only barely. This whole thing had him rattled, too. Maybe it was more than just a new murder case? I let out a slow breath, my mind already working. Something about this felt off. And I had a sinking feeling Liza's murder was just the beginning.

Behind us a shout rang out—a sharp, urgent voice calling for Chase. We turned in unison. One of the deputies standing near Liza's body, gestured frantically. "Sheriff! You need to see this."

Chase shot me a look, warning me to stay back, before jogging to the scene. Obviously, he knew by now I wasn't going to listen. I stepped closer anyway, my pulse hammering in my ears. Deputy Liam Caldwell knelt beside Liza's belongings, carefully pulling at a crumpled piece of paper. I couldn't read the words, but I saw one thing clearly: Misty's name, scrawled in bold ink.

"Good work, Liam. You need to bag that and everything else there. Gary's calling in the team from Port Byron. Until they get here, start roping off the crime scene."

"Got it, Sir."

Chase continued onward, shouting orders and pushing spectators back. My mind raced and my breath caught in my chest. Whatever was on that paper wasn't good.

Five

The crime scene had barely been roped off before Scallywag made his move. One moment, the coroner Rip was crouched over Liza's body, and the next, a flurry of blue and gold swooped down from nowhere, landing on a low tree branch just above Chase's head.

"Half-baked! Half-baked!" Scallywag screeched, flapping his wings and bobbing his head.

The gathered crowd gasped. Chase jabbed his finger in the air at the fractious fowl. "That parrot is going to land himself in a holding cell."

"Oh, no!" I cried as Major appeared, barking wildly. The over-sized sheepdog lunged toward the tree, front paws scraping against the trunk as he jumped, spun, and barked at his feathered rival.

"Where did he come from?" Chase asked, scanning the area.

Oliver burst through the trees, panting. "I'm sorry, Chase, he broke away from me when Scallywag flew by. I've been chasing him all the way here."

Scallywag hopped to a higher branch, cackling. "Eeeek! Too late now! Too late!"

Chase mumbled what I assumed was a curse word. "Juli, grab Major before he makes this worse!"

"I tried, but he won't stop moving!" I lunged for the dog again, but he just escaped my grasp.

These two had always been trouble together, and today was no exception. Scallywag, clearly enjoying the chaos, dove from the tree, soaring over the festival booths. Major, focused and determined to catch the feisty fowl, took off after him. He zigzagged through the crime scene, knocking over a small evidence marker and sending a stack of festival programs flying.

"Major!" Chase yelled as we watched his shaggy deputy drag parts of the crime tape behind him like a victory banner.

"Scallywag, get back here you naughty bird!" I shouted to no avail.

"C'mon, let's go." When Chase reached out his hand, I instinctively took it and we began to run, following the path of destruction left behind by the conniving culprits.

We caught up to the dastardly duo as we dodged festivalgoers and accidentally toppled a basket of candied apples in the process. Thank goodness they were individually wrapped. Scallywag dipped low, skimming the grass at the edge of the path. He touched down long enough to snatch up a crumpled piece of paper in his beak.

"Drop it!" I shouted as I broke away from Chase, sprinting ahead to dive at the bird.

Scallywag screeched and dropped the paper midair. It drifted softly to the ground like the falling leaves, settling close to where I landed beside a hay bale. Chase skidded to a stop and helped me up while I victoriously held the wad of paper in my fingers.

"Are you okay?" he asked, and I nodded, trying to catch my breath. "What is that?" He rested his hand on my shoulder and leaned in as I slowly opened the paper. We smoothed out the wrinkled page and my stomach flipped.

It was a festival schedule. Misty's name was circled right next to the exact time she had set out her desserts.

Chase's jaw tightened. "This isn't good."

I swallowed hard as recognition dawned. "This is the second clue. Someone planned this."

We exchanged a look before taking the schedule in as evidence. Only the crazy canine and his feathered accomplice weren't finished. By the time we had bagged the crumpled schedule, the parrot had led Major on a wild chase around the festival, barreling through a popcorn stand and causing a near pile-up at the pumpkin patch.

I almost caught Scallywag in mid-flight near the cider stand, but he saw me coming and looped through a scarecrow display. A group of young girls screamed as the giant bird flew low over their heads. Chase lunged for Major's leash near the hayride, but Major dodged at the last second, sending Chase face-first into a pile of loose straw.

We cornered them near the ring toss booth, but Scallywag took off again, squawking, "It's the cops!"

"Woof-Woof-Howwwl!" Major sounded off like a siren as he raced after Scallywag.

Chase glared at me. "I swear that bird is part demon."

I stifled a laugh. "Welcome to my world."

We continued our pursuit through town. By the time we reached Mrs. Bailey's house, we were both winded and covered in festival debris. Scallywag soared through an open window and perched effortlessly on his stand like he hadn't just terrorized half the town. Major, finally caught, collapsed on the grass at our feet, panting but pleased.

Chase and I locked eyes and for a second, the frustration melted into something else. Something familiar. I brushed the fronts of my jeans then reached toward him.

"You're looking more like a cowboy than a lawman with all

this hay in your hair." I giggled while flicking the golden shafts off his head.

"Look who's talking, you still have blue feathers sticking out of yours." His solid laugh and gleam in his eyes while he plucked remnants of Scallywag from my hair did funny things to my insides. He stepped closer, his eyes zeroing in on my mouth.

I swallowed hard.

Then, just as fast, Chase cleared his throat and took a deliberate step back. "Thanks for your help getting them home."

I nodded quickly, not sure what was or wasn't happening. "Right. Of course. Do you have to get back to the crime scene?"

"Gary's got it covered. Been a long day. I've got a date with a pile of paperwork."

I nodded once, at a loss for words. So much for my cider date.

The air still hummed between us as we turned and walked separately into our houses. When I stepped through the door, Oliver was waiting.

"I'm surprised to see you here. I thought for sure you would be with Misty," I said, eyeing him carefully.

He frowned. "I would be, but she said she wants to be alone to process everything. Something's been off with her lately." He shrugged. "Don't worry about me...you and Chase looked awfully cozy at the festival," he said, leaning against the door jam. He extended his arm, stopping me in my tracks. "I've got to tell you, you look an absolute wreck right now."

I sighed, rubbing my temples. "Not now, Oliver. I need a shower."

But he wasn't letting it go. Following me through the house he said, "Juli...what's really going on with you and the sheriff?"

I paused at the base of the stairs, opening my mouth to speak then closed it tight. All I could do was shrug. I had no good answer.

I DESCENDED THE STAIRS HALF AN HOUR LATER, FEELING cozy in my Boston Celtics lounge pants and matching hoodie. I expected Oliver to be sitting on the couch, waiting to corner me about Chase. Instead, he stood by the window, hands in his pockets.

"Chase stopped by," he said before I could speak. "Said he owes you a conversation. Wanted me to tell you to come over whenever you're ready. Said his door will be open."

My pulse jumped. I tucked a damp strand of hair behind my ear. "Did he say what about?"

Oliver turned, giving me one of those 'come on, really?' looks. "What do you think?" He started toward the hallway. "I'm going to bed."

"Oliver—"

"Just talk to him, Jules. Figure it out," he said over his shoulder before disappearing upstairs.

I hesitated a beat longer, then grabbed a bottle of wine from the counter and a throw blanket from the arm of the couch. Chase did owe me a conversation, and I wanted that talk. Maybe more than I cared to admit.

His living room was warm and inviting, and it smelled faintly of cedar and spice. The fireplace crackled steadily, the flames flickering across the dark stone hearth. His worn leather couch sat angled toward the growing warmth, a knit blanket draped over the arm. The coffee table was pushed aside, replaced with two thick floor cushions. Clearly, he'd planned for this.

I set my wine and blanket down, easing onto one of the cushions and stretching my legs toward the fire. I let the heat seep into my skin, drawing comfort from the way it seemed to chase the day's tension away.

The faint thud of footsteps sounded from upstairs. A moment later, Chase appeared at the top of the steps in a pair of gray sweats and an unbuttoned flannel shirt, his hair still damp and tousled from his shower. My stomach did a weird little flip.

"Hey," he said, a lazy smile curling his lips. "Hope you're hungry. I ordered Falafel Oasis before I got in the shower. It's in the kitchen, I'll go grab the plates." He gestured toward the direction of the kitchen and disappeared.

"I brought wine," I called after him. "Bring some glasses, too."

"Perfect," he said from the kitchen. A moment later, he returned with wine glasses in one hand and a tray loaded with salad, falafel wraps, hummus, and pita in the other. He placed the tray between us and sat down on the cushion next to mine.

"I wasn't sure if you'd come," he said after a moment.

"Neither was I," I admitted. "But...I'm glad I did." I glanced down at all my favorites, my heart warming. "So, the Oasis won you over? I'll make a vegetarian out of you yet." I grabbed a plate and spooned a large serving of tabbouleh salad with a side of hummus and pita.

"Let's not get too carried away." The smile that reached his eyes brought me back to center. "I'll admit having tried it a couple more times since the fair. I have to say it's a refreshing option from cheeseburgers and pizza."

"That's all I can ask for." This was what I needed. What I'd been missing. Our friendship was special. It always had been.

He smiled, then grabbed a falafel wrap and took a bite. "Okay," he said through a mouthful, "let's talk."

I poured the wine and handed him a glass. "I want to help," I said, watching him closely. "With the investigation."

"Juli..."

"I know Misty didn't do this," I pressed. "We both know she's not capable of something like this."

He wiped his hands on a napkin, his expression serious. "I get it. But until I figure out who else had it in for Liza, Misty's still the main suspect."

"There has to be more," I insisted. "What about the notes we found?"

"The team is processing them. They'll look for prints, analyze the handwriting."

"Then we need to put our heads together." I finished my wine and Chase refilled both our glasses.

"What about Boston?" he asked after setting the bottle down.

I arched a brow. "What about it?"

"Think about it, Oliver arrives in town and now the woman he's pursuing is accused of murder."

I hesitated. "Do you think Liza had ties to Boston, too?" I'd spent years in that city, trying to build a life while working at the art gallery. Maybe trouble had found Liza like it had found me?

"I don't know," Chase admitted. "But I'm going to find out."

I met his gaze, biting my lip. "It's not connected. I swear."

He studied me for a moment before nodding. "I believe you."

Silence settled between us, broken only by the soft pop of the fire. Finally, I gathered my courage. "Chase, where does this leave us?"

His eyes softened. "You tell me."

I scoffed. "I don't know. You've been acting weird ever since..."

"Since April started showing an interest in me again?" he cut in, grinning like the devil. "You're still jealous."

"She didn't just start to show an interest in you, Chase. She's liked you since forever, and you know it. As far as jealous?" I snorted. "You're the one who should be jealous. I finally agreed to have cider with Gary at the festival." He didn't have to know it got cancelled by a little thing called murder.

"Did you now?" He leaned closer, his grin widening. "Sounds like you're trying to make me jealous."

"Maybe," I teased.

His gaze lingered briefly on my lips, and for a second, I thought he might kiss me. Instead, he reached for his wine, taking a long sip before setting the glass aside.

"I'm trying, Juli," he said quietly. "I'm trying to be patient. But this...whatever this is between us...it's not nothing. It never has been."

"I know," I whispered. "And I'm trying, too. Tonight...means a lot. I've missed this."

We fell quiet again, the easy kind of quiet that felt warm and familiar. I shifted closer, tossing the blanket over both of us. Chase leaned back against the couch, one arm draped loosely around my shoulder.

"You're not going to ditch me for Gary, are you?" he murmured.

"Might," I teased, resting my head against his shoulder. Boy, did this feel so right. I felt like I could stay here forever. So why didn't I? Why couldn't I open up and tell him what I found out so many years ago, what really drove me away and what I was still afraid of?

He chuckled low, the sound vibrating against me. "You're trouble, Scarlett."

"And you love it." I smiled even though he couldn't see.

"Yeah," he said softly. "I really do."

And I really had to be sure where we stood before speaking my truth and risk losing everything.

The bottle of wine dwindled, our plates emptied, and the warmth of the fire lulled me into a comfortable haze. I barely registered my head sliding down onto Chase's chest before sleep claimed me.

It was morning when the faint sound of a car door slamming outside jolted me awake. I blinked groggily, the dim glow of the fire revealing Chase still asleep beside me. His arm lay loosely around my waist, his chest rising and falling in a steady rhythm.

I shifted carefully, trying not to wake him, but his eyes flickered open.

"What time is it?" he mumbled, his voice heavy with sleep. The sharp knock at the front door brought him instantly awake.

"I'll get it," I offered, but he shook his head, already pushing himself upright.

"No," he said firmly. "Stay here."

He crossed the room in a few long strides and disappeared down the hall. The quiet stretch before the door opened felt too long, and unease prickled at my skin. Something about the way Chase's shoulders had squared told me that whatever news waited outside...it wasn't good.

"What's wrong?" I asked once the door was closed. I followed him into the kitchen, my stomach a ball of nerves. He was quiet. Too quiet. The coffee had already brewed, thank God, and he didn't say a word until he'd poured both of our cups and added cream to mine.

"We have a print match on one of the notes we found." Chase took a long drink from his cup.

"Who?" I set my cup on the counter, untouched, my worry meter coming alive. "Please don't say it was Misty."

"Claire Bennett."

Six

After sharing another cup of coffee, I crossed between the arborvitaes to my house. I still couldn't believe the police had Claire's fingerprints from one of the notes. Chase had sworn me to secrecy, not to say a word until he had a chance to question her. Since he was in a hurry to get to the station, we promised to meet up later and I planned to tell him about my conversation with Claire before joining him to talk to her. There had to be a logical explanation.

Right now, Oliver and I needed to check on Misty. As we made our way to the *Sunflower Inn*, he ran a hand through his already mussed hair, the crisp autumn air doing little to cool his obvious frustration.

"Did you see him with her? He couldn't keep his hands off her," Oliver huffed, flinging his arms in the air. His usual easygoing charm was nowhere to be found. Instead, irritation burned in his brown eyes, his mouth set in a firm line. "The way she clung to him, Jules, like she needed him. Like Ethan Harris was the only person who could make her feel safe. I should have been the one comforting her."

I sighed. "They are old friends, Ollie. Of course he's going to be there for her."

"Yeah? Well, I've been helping her with everything at the inn. I've been here. Where the heck was he?"

"He doesn't live in New Hope. I was told he visits his parents often and helps Misty whenever he can. You can't fault him for that."

"Actually, I'd prefer to." He sighed heavily. "You saw him, Jules, he's a handsome guy and I have to compete with that. He looked ready to fight Chase last night right then and there. Like Misty belonged to him. This is exactly what he wants. A chance to be her champion."

I pressed my lips together, considering that statement. Ethan had looked awfully at home holding Misty last night, and even now the thought spurred to life my worry meter. But the way she had melted against him...had there been something in her expression? Some part of her that needed him more than she had admitted to me?

"Don't get crazy over this. Honestly, I get it." I chose my words carefully. "You like her, and you don't want to feel like you're second choice. Are you sure she really knows how you feel? Have you come right out and told her?"

Oliver released a pent-up breath, his expression stormy. "For crying out loud, Jules, I wear my heart on my sleeve. She has to know."

Before I could argue, the front door to the inn opened, and Misty stepped out onto the porch. Her normally cheerful eyes darted around, wary, and her shoulders tensed when she saw us. "Hey," she said, her voice hoarse. She lifted her coffee mug to her lips, but I noticed she barely drank. The dark circles under her eyes looked worse this morning, as if she hadn't slept at all.

Oliver stepped in close, lowering his voice. "Misty, did you get any rest?"

She gave a half-hearted smile. "Tried." Then rubbed her temple. "Didn't work."

Ethan appeared from around the corner, a tool belt slung over his shoulder and his brow furrowed. "You didn't sleep at all," he said sending her a knowing look as he walked up the porch steps, then addressed Oliver and me. "I told her I'd stay at the inn last night. Just in case she needed anything."

Oliver stiffened beside me, his arms crossing. "That's...considerate of you." I could tell he was wounded that he'd made the same offer only to have Misty tell him she wanted to be alone to process everything.

Ethan's expression was unreadable, but I caught the shift in his stance, a subtle movement that spoke volumes. He wasn't just there to help. He was there to protect her. And by the way Misty shared her coffee cup, she wasn't pushing him away.

"Who do you think is actually trying to frame you?" I asked carefully. "It had to be someone who knew when you were setting out that cobbler. Someone close."

Misty let out a breath, her voice wavering. "I don't know, Juli. But whoever did this...they knew exactly how to make it look like it was me. And it's working." She rested her face in her hands. "This is a nightmare," she said, exasperation evident in her voice. "I didn't poison Liza. I have to figure out who would want to ruin me."

Ethan still had a hand on her back while he took another sip of coffee. His gaze, sharp and unwavering, swept over the small crowd heading toward Miller Park for the start of the day's activities. "Whoever did this had a plan," he said. "And they were watching. That means they're still here."

I frowned, my mind flashing back to Claire's wounded expression last night. She had every reason to resent Misty. But could she have taken it this far? I thought about our conversation after the bake-off. The jealousy in her voice, the way she had watched Misty and Oliver together. Could she have poisoned Liza? Was Misty right about being framed?

I kept the thought to myself. Not until I could talk to Chase.

———

LATER THAT AFTERNOON, CHASE AND I STEPPED INTO *Ringo's Diner.* Vinnie Minetti could be heard barking orders back in the kitchen as the packed diner confirmed a very busy Fall Festival weekend. I'd left the inn with enough time to spare to enlighten Chase on my conversation with Claire.

"You shouldn't have to come. I'm capable of interviewing a person of interest on my own." He took my coat and hung it on a hook just inside the door. "Why don't you find a spot at the counter, and I'll call you over when I'm done with Claire."

"No way, Lawman."

"Juli..." his voice rumbled a warning that by now he knew darn well I was going to ignore.

"First of all." I raised my index finger. "You're going to come off all 'by the book' and the poor girl is going to feel like you're accusing her of murder."

"Hey, she very well could replace Misty as a suspect, considering everything you've told me. She could have committed the murder."

"Yes, but you don't have to make her think that we think so."

"Last I looked, Ms. Butler, you don't have a badge or a J.D. in law."

"And last I knew, I've been very beneficial to you in solving the last two cases that have happened under your command." I fought to control a smile when Chase's green eyes narrowed in amused scrutiny. "Which brings me to point number two." I held up two fingers for emphasis.

"Go on," he encouraged, and I didn't miss the slight pull at the corners of his mouth.

"If I'm at the table with you, Claire may relax and feel like she can be honest about everything."

"Possibly."

"You willing to take that chance?" I nodded toward the booth where Claire Bennett sat alone. "She's already seen us together. It would look weird if you left me behind."

"Or it would look like I'm doing my job." He stepped forward first and tapped my elbow. "C'mon. But I do the talking, got it?"

"Of course, Captain Do-Good."

"It's Sheriff."

"Whatever." I groaned, then smiled brightly when we reached the table.

"Juli, Chase. What's going on?" Claire glanced up from the menu as we approached, her expression immediately guarded. Chase slid into the booth across from her, and I took the seat next to him.

"We need to talk about Liza," I said before Chase could speak. His knee knocked painfully against mine and I tried to cover my wince by reaching for a menu.

Claire's hand tightened around her coffee mug. "What about her?"

I exchanged a glance with Chase before jumping in. "We know you were at the bake-off," I continued. "And we know you were watching Misty and Oliver."

Her cheeks flushed. "That doesn't mean anything."

Chase raised an eyebrow. "So, you weren't upset about Misty getting all of Oliver's attention?"

Claire's lips pressed together. "I—" She stopped short, her eyes locking on me. "I can't believe you told him. I should never have confided in you, but you are Oliver's friend, and I trusted you."

"You can trust me, Claire. We're just trying to rule out anyone who could have had motive for setting up Misty Shepard."

"Look, I won't lie. It stung seeing them together. But that doesn't mean I poisoned Liza."

I studied her carefully. She looked flustered but not guilty. Still, I wasn't convinced.

Chase cleared his throat. "We have your prints on part of a festival schedule with Misty's name circled along with the time she would be putting out her display."

"Do I need a lawyer?" Claire's eyes darted to each of us, and I noticed fear creeping into her features.

"If there's something you want to tell us, we can continue this conversation at the station," Chase added, all business-like and this time it was my knee that thwacked his.

"What he's saying," I gently added, "is that while this appears incriminating, based on your actions, we're just gathering information. If there are things you think might help the case, we, I mean Chase, can take a formal statement back in his office."

"Of course I had a schedule." Claire's tone shifted to annoyance. "And yes, I had circled Misty's name. To be honest, I wasn't there to see her. I was hoping I'd have a chance to see Oliver again. I waited around, but he never showed up, so I left."

"That's all we need to know," I said, keeping my focus firmly on Claire and refusing to acknowledge the long, knowing look I could feel Chase directing my way.

"I'm assuming you've questioned Misty, too?" Claire paused until she was sure she had our attention. "Liza was a real threat to her, and she was really eager to get in on the negotiations if the inn went up for sale."

"What do you mean?" I glanced from Chase to Claire. "The inn is fine. Misty is working on fixing everything."

Claire ripped open a sugar packet and poured it into her mug. "Rumor has it she's fallen behind on payments. Liza knew that."

"I always thought her parents owned it outright." Chase scratched at his stubbled chin.

"I have friends at the bank who say she borrowed against the place. Lord knows what she's been doing with all that money."

"Certainly not making repairs," I mused out loud and Chase's knee found mine once again. "Ow!"

"All I'm saying is," Claire raised her voice, "I'm the least of your concerns. I may be interested in Oliver, but I certainly wouldn't kill for him."

Chase leaned back, watching her for a moment before tapping me on the hip to leave. "We'll be in touch."

"Hey, Butler," Vinnie yelled from behind the counter as we walked by, "thanks for stealing my best server."

"Sorry, Vin, I offered Scott a deal he couldn't refuse." I waved and Vinnie shook his head.

"What was that all about?" Chase asked as we walked out of the diner.

"Andie Evans. I hired her after I opened the café. Then I found out she and Scott Iverson were dating so I hired him to work for me, too. I thought it would be a good way for them to spend more time together instead of working different shifts. Scott thought it was great. Vinnie? Not so much."

"Who knew you were a matchmaker?" Chase tapped my nose. "Nice job letting me handle the conversation in there, by the way."

"Sorry. I couldn't help myself. I figured if I did the talking, you could watch her like the trained detective that you are."

"Sheriff. I'm a sheriff."

"Whatever, Lawman." I stopped walking and turned to him. "What did you think?"

He sighed. "I think she's hiding something. We just don't know what. But I do know I need to look into the financial state of the inn. I've heard some grumbling about Victor Langley. Maybe that's why he's been seen around town. He's got a reputation for being ruthless when it comes to buying out failing businesses or rundown properties."

And that was enough to keep Claire firmly on my suspect list, along with educating myself on Victor Langley.

Seven

Day three of the festival and I'd finally been able to confirm time with Gary. I wiped my hands on my apron, taking a step back from my Barking for Apples booth as he approached. We wandered from booth to booth. Enticing aromas of roasted nuts, caramel apples and warm cider drifted through the air. People laughed and chatted as they played games and sampled local treats. It was the kind of picturesque fall day that should have made me feel lighter, but there was a weight hanging over me that even the festival's charm couldn't lift.

"Finally," Gary said, giving my arm a slight nudge. "I get you to myself for a little bit. I was starting to think you were avoiding me."

I shot him a side glance. "You're determined, I'll give you that."

He placed a dramatic hand over his heart as he led me toward O'Toole's food stand. "It's one of my best qualities." Jimmy and Tammy owned the fish market, and she always made amazing seafood dishes to sell at the counter. We stopped to peruse the chalkboard menu boasting New England Clam Chowder, Lobster Bisque, and Homemade Cornbread. "Along with my impeccable timing and the fact that I know how much you like your chowder. And you did say yes to dinner, cider, or something."

"How could I forget?" I laughed despite myself. "Alright, I'll bite. What else should I know about Deputy Maxwell?"

Gary eagerly smiled, handing me my bowl of steaming chowder and leading me to an empty park bench. "Well, I'm a good listener. And I ask the questions people don't want to answer." He turned his head slightly, his hazel eyes studying me. "Like...what's really going on with you and Chase?"

The warmth of the chowder suddenly wasn't enough to chase away the chill curling in my stomach. I blew out a breath and glanced at him. "You don't beat around the bush, do you?"

"Not my style," he said before devouring a generous spoonful of potatoes and clams. "But," he swallowed, "I don't ask just to be nosy. I genuinely care. And I want to know, in turn, where I stand."

I stirred my chowder, turning my attention to the trees, their red and orange leaves appearing more vibrant in the afternoon sun. "Chase and I...we're complicated."

Gary scoffed. "Understatement of the year."

I let out a small chuckle. "We have a history. A messy one at that. Neither of us has figured out how to maneuver through it."

"Do you want to move forward?" Gary asked, his voice softer as he leaned his forearms on his thighs.

That was the question. I rubbed my fingers over the edge of the chowder cup. "I don't know." I met the sincerity in his eyes. "Some days, it feels like we're getting somewhere. Other days, it's like we're just going in circles."

Gary nodded thoughtfully, taking a slow sip of his chowder. "I can respect that. I just need to know if I'm waiting for something that is never going to happen."

"Gary, I don't want to lead you on. I think you're a great guy. To be honest, I don't have all the answers right now."

He studied me for a moment, then smiled, though there was a

hint of something unreadable in his eyes. "I appreciate that." He nudged my knee with his. "And just so we're clear—I'm a patient guy."

The tension between us eased into something lighter, something comfortable. I opened my mouth to respond when a sharp voice from behind us snagged my attention.

"A very difficult woman," Victor Langley spoke into his phone, his tone laced with irritation. "It's a good thing I didn't have to step in. I wasn't too keen on working with that Blake woman to begin with."

Gary and I both went still, our conversation forgotten as we turned slightly toward the sound of Langley's voice. He stood tall, his coat open exposing a dress shirt and a pair of black pants and boots. He reminded me of a wealthy rancher, minus the cowboy hat. His short, salt and pepper hair and mustache gave him an edge, bringing to mind what Chase had mentioned about his business dealings. Langley paced near the vendor stalls, his phone pressed to his ear, oblivious to the fact we were in earshot.

"Of course, it's better this way," Langley continued. "She would have made things far more difficult than necessary."

I exchanged a look with Gary, my worry meter humming with each knot in my stomach. This wasn't just casual business talk. Langley was referring to Liza. And from the way he was talking, he was relieved she was gone.

Gary straightened, his chowder forgotten. "I'll look into Langley," he said under his breath. "Fill in Chase."

I nodded, still listening as Langley continued speaking into his phone before walking away. My mind raced. Liza had been difficult, sure. But had she been difficult enough for someone to want her dead? Possibly even Victor Langley?

Gary stood, stretching before turning to face me. "I meant what I said earlier," he added, his tone softer now, "I don't mind being patient, Juli. But I don't intend to sit on the sidelines forever."

I glanced up at him, my heart doing something strange and unfamiliar. Before I could find the right words, he winked and walked off toward the festival booths, leaving me alone with my thoughts and a bowl of chowder that had suddenly lost all its appeal.

———

TOWARD THE END OF THE DAY, I STOPPED BY *Henderson's Hardware,* looking for more twine to secure a fresh batch of treats to the floating apples at my booth. The bell over the door jingled as I stepped inside, the scent of sawdust and motor oil thick in the air. Rows of neatly stocked shelves held everything from nails to garden hoses.

I was browsing near the back when I saw Walter and Mabel Harris. Ethan's parents, by the paint display, speaking in hushed tones. I never really knew them because Ethan was older, and I never remembered my mother mentioning them. Their secretiveness in the store was enough to garner my attention. I pretended to inspect a spool of twine while keeping one ear on their conversation.

"...all taken care of," Walter said, voice low, "No more problems."

Mabel huffed, her arms crossed over her chest. "You say that, but now there's all this attention. If we'd just waited—"

Walter's tone became short as he raked his fingers through his graying hair. "It had to be done. We couldn't afford to let things drag on."

I stiffened. The way they spoke sent a prickle down my spine. Were they talking about Liza? About Misty? Or something else entirely?

I reached for a spool of twine, making a show of examining the price tag as Mabel's gaze scanned in my direction. Her expression immediately shifted into something more neutral. "Well, if it isn't

Julianna Butler," she said, plastering on a tight smile. "Haven't ever seen you in here before."

Walter turned, his gaze sharp but unreadable. "Hello there. Everything all right?"

I forced an easy smile. "I practically lived here when I first came back to town. Between opening my café and adding my own touches to the house, I've been keeping busy fixing things. Today, I'm just picking up some supplies for the festival." I held up the spool of twine.

Walter chuckled as he shoved his hands in his pockets and rocked back on his heels. "Your daddy knew how to fix anything—not just machines either. He knew how to keep a secret tighter than a stripped bolt."

"Walter!" Mabel gasped.

The older man shrugged. "What? It's true."

I frowned. "What kind of secrets?" My dad could never keep a secret from me and mom. He cracked under pressure every time.

"Oh ...just the kind folks used to take to the grave. Different world back then." He stooped to pick up a roll of electrical tape.

I kept my tone light. "I'm sure it was."

"Speaking of graves." Mabel's smile thinned. "It's a shame about Liza, of course. But these things have a way of working themselves out."

Walter nodded. "Best to let the professionals do their job."

There was something off about the way he said it, like he was warning me to keep my nose out of it. "Of course," I said, feigning nonchalance. "Anyway, I should get going. Enjoy the rest of your day."

At the counter, I spotted Betty Henderson, who was bagging a customer's items with her usual no-nonsense efficiency.

"Hello there, darlin'. Find everything you needed?" She cheerfully smiled when I set my items on the counter.

"Betty," I asked casually, "what can you tell me about the Harris family?"

She gave me a confused look. "Walter and Mabel? Absolutely wonderful people. That family has been part of New Hope for generations. I'm sure if you ever wanted to know about the history of New Hope they would love to talk your ear off." Betty lowered her voice, peeking toward the aisles. "Seriously, doll, those old timers love to talk. I gotta look busy up here or they will stick around 'til closing time, jawing away! Just ask Harry."

"Oh dear."

"They are still wandering around the store if you want to talk to them."

"That's all right. I didn't remember them at first," I said, summoning a smile. "Ethan is older, and we never really hung out."

"That's right! Another wonderful young man. They did a fine job raising him, even though they were older when he was born. That Misty would be a fool if she didn't latch on to that boy before he gives up trying."

"Right," I said as I collected my change, one hundred percent reading into the Misty-Ethan inference as if she were referring to me and Gary. It wouldn't surprise me if small town gossip was already spreading about Gary and me on a park bench sharing chowder.

As I stepped out of the store, a cold unease settled over me. I didn't know what the Harris' were up to, but I was determined to find out. And now I had more information for Chase.

First, I needed to skirt down the street and pick up some mini peanut butter bones Andie had texted me that were ready. I walked through the door of my café just as Chase was stepping up to the counter. He turned, a smile already forming along with a teasing twinkle in his eyes. "Hey, stranger."

I set my bag of hardware store supplies down with a sigh. "Hey yourself. Busy day?"

"Always. Time to fuel up." He leaned an elbow against the counter. "Had an interesting conversation with Gary earlier."

I arched a brow. "Oh?"

"Yeah." Chase took his coffee from Mark and took a sip before continuing. "He filled me in on your little eavesdropping session at the park this afternoon."

"It wasn't eavesdropping. It was—"

"Strategic listening?" he supplied, amusement dancing in his eyes.

"Exactly." I agreed only because I was wondering if Gary said anything else to Chase...like how he was being patient, or whatever it is guys would say to each other.

Chase shook his head. "You're going to get yourself into trouble."

"Something like that," I mumbled then quickly changed the direction of our conversation. "Not if you solve this case before I do," I shot back with a playful edge to my voice. "And speaking of that, when are you free to talk?"

He hesitated, rubbing the back of his neck. "Can't tonight. I promised April I'd take a look at her fuse box."

My smile faltered, and something shifted in Chase's expression —like he knew exactly the direction my mind was taking it. "You're adorable when you're jealous," he teased.

"I'm not jealous."

"Uh-huh." He cast a lopsided grin, taking another slow sip of his coffee.

I folded my arms. "I just find it interesting that you always seem to be at April's beck and call."

He chuckled, setting his cup down. "Juli, I promise you, fixing a fuse box is not my idea of an exciting evening." His voice softened. "Tomorrow. We'll talk then."

That seemed to settle something inside me, but I wasn't about to let him off the hook that easily. "Fine. But if she starts asking you to put up shelves, I'm revoking your handyman privileges."

Chase laughed, shaking his head. "Noted." Then his expression sobered. "Mayor Montgomery's been on me about finding the killer. She wants a named suspect. Soon."

I frowned. "That's ridiculous. You can't rush an investigation just because the mayor wants it wrapped up in a neat little bow."

"Try telling her that." Chase let out a slow breath. "She's pushing hard. And I have a feeling if I don't produce some solid leads, she's going to make my life miserable."

I reached out, placing a hand on his arm. "You'll figure this out, Chase. You always do."

He looked down at where my hand rested against his sleeve, then back up at me, his expression hard to read. "Yeah. With a little help from you, no doubt."

The air between us thickened, something unspoken hovering just beneath the surface. Then he exhaled, shaking his head, a faint flicker of amusement playing across his lips. "Major misses you, by the way."

I grinned. "Oh, does he?"

"Yep. Keeps looking for you every time I come through the door. Then lays by the door and mopes like I've let him down."

"Smart dog," I said, grabbing a napkin and scribbling something down, "tell my buddy I'm free for a walk tomorrow. We'll grab dinner on the way home."

Chase took the napkin, his fingers brushing mine for half a second longer than necessary. "Sounds good. I'll let him know." I watched him peek at my scribbled attempt at being romantic, smiling at my cryptic 🤍 C+J+🐾🐾 🤍.

As he turned to leave, I let out a breath I hadn't realized I was holding. I didn't know what was going to happen between us, but one thing was certain—tomorrow couldn't come fast enough.

Eight

The next day, I decided to forgo the festival and catch up on things at *The Butler's Pantry* and *Petite Four Paws Cafe*. The place was packed with Leaf Peepers, tourists drawn in by the festival and the brilliant colors of the changing trees. The aroma of freshly baked maple scones and spiced lattes filled the cozy space as I made my way behind the counter, thankful for Oliver's help rolling out peanut butter dough for the next batch of dog treats.

"Busy day," he commented, nodding toward the crowd.

"Tell me about it," I said, grabbing a basket of muffins to restock the pastry case. "I'm glad you're here. I thought for sure you'd be helping Misty at her booth or the inn."

Oliver hesitated, then pulled something from his pocket—a small, plain envelope.

"This was waiting for me at the registration desk at the inn," he said, handing it over.

I frowned, flipping it over. "No return address?"

"Yeah," he said grimly. "Because whoever sent it doesn't want to be found."

I pulled out the note inside. It was typed.

I know what you took. You can't hide forever.

I looked up sharply. "You think it's about your sculpture?"

Oliver nodded. "I think someone followed me here from Boston. The only people who know I have it are you, Amelia and Nando. So, someone else had to have seen us that night."

My stomach dropped. "Oliver—"

"I know," he said quickly. "I know what you're going to say. But the damage is done."

I breathed deep, pinching the bridge of my nose. I had already been in hot water with Chase about my Boston past. I had promised him there were no more skeletons.

Now this?

Sure, my friends and I compensated ourselves with artwork for services we were never paid for. David knew and had basically let it go after realizing the error of his ways and all of the trouble he wanted to avoid. Especially now that he was back at the gallery and things were going well with Rita and him.

I swallowed hard. "What exactly do they know? Do you have any idea who it could be?"

Oliver tensed. "I don't know. But they left this for a reason."

And that reason wasn't good. I motioned for Oliver to follow me to my back office. We closed the door, the hum of voices from the front muffled by the walls. The envelope sat between us like a loaded gun.

"We need to come clean to Chase," I said finally.

Oliver threw himself back in the chair. "And tell him what? That I stole a priceless sculpture from the gallery? That someone's tracked me here?"

I crossed my arms. "It's not just someone, Oliver. Whoever sent this note isn't playing games. Chase has an idea of what happened at the gallery."

Oliver leaned forward. "And what happens when we tell Chase? You really think he's going to look the other way?"

I hesitated. No. No, I didn't.

Oliver's jaw tightened. "You promised him there were no more skeletons, right? What do you think happens when he finds out that isn't true?"

I forced a swallow. Ollie wasn't wrong. Chase had already lost trust in me once. If I went to him now...if he found out I'd kept this from him—

"Look," Oliver said, his voice lower now. "We keep quiet. We figure out who sent this. If it gets worse, we reassess things."

I bit my lip. My worry meter setting off alarms in my head, my palms damp with the sweat of deceit. "And if it gets worse too fast?"

Oliver's gaze darkened. "Then we run."

My breath caught. Every time something got bad, I would run from my problems. But that was my past. I couldn't do that again. Not to Chase. Not after everything.

"Don't worry, Jules," Oliver said, softer now and obviously seeing the fear on my face. "You're not ready to burn that bridge. Not yet."

I shook my head. "I hate this."

He gave a humorless laugh. "Yeah. Well, that's our last resort. First, we figure out who it is, what they really want, and we deal with it on our own. Okay?"

"Oliver, I wouldn't risk this for anyone else, you know that."

"And I love you for it. Welcome to my life."

I stared down at the note, heart pounding. Coming clean might ruin everything. But keeping quiet?

I didn't dare think about how worse it could get.

———

THE EVENING AIR WAS BRISK AS I WALKED MAJOR HOME from the dog park, his leash loose in my hand as he happily trotted beside me. The golden leaves crunched underfoot, and the streetlights flickered on, casting a warm glow along Main Street.

As we passed *Ringo's Diner*, I gave Major's head a quick scratch. "What do you think, boy? Should we bring home some dinner?" His whole body wiggled and bumped against my leg, which I took as a yes. I looped his leash around a bike stand. "Stay. I'll be right back."

Inside, the scent of grilled burgers filled the air along with Vinnie's famous sauce and the buzz of casual conversation as families gathered in retro booths for their dinner. I stepped up to the counter where Vinnie grinned at me. "Juli, good to see you. Usual?"

"Not tonight," I said, scanning the menu. "I'll take a double cheeseburger for Chase, a veggie burger for me, and a double order of sweet potato fries."

Vinnie chuckled, ringing up the order. "Chase is a lucky guy."

I bit the inside of my cheek, not sure how to respond. Luckily, Major spied me through the door and barked, distracting me from having to answer. A few minutes later, with dinner in hand, I made another stop at *Sally's Sweet Treats*. The bell over the door jingled as I stepped inside, the air thick with the scent of chocolate and vanilla. Sally Sweet, the shop's owner, beamed at me from behind the counter. Sally was a petite woman with lavender eyes and short, silver hair. She started the business with her husband Randy, and it had been a town staple since I was old enough to tag along with my parents.

"Juli! What can I get you?"

"I need a bag of those sea salt caramels. Chase is obsessed with them," I said, scanning the display case filled with delicate pastries and handmade confections.

"One of my best sellers." Sally grinned as she grabbed a small bag and tied it with a purple plaid ribbon. "That man has good taste. How's he holding up with everything?"

I sighed. "He's stretched thin but determined to figure this out. I plan on helping him as long as he'll let me."

Sally's expression softened. "Good. If there's anything I can do to help, you let me know."

"Thanks, Sally. I'll let Chase know." I paused a beat, then asked, "Does Sierra know about Liza? Are they still close?" Sierra Sweet and Liza had been best friends back in high school.

"Heavens no! They had a falling out right after college. She's across the country in Sacramento working on a line of athletic wear. My girl is finally making a name for herself."

Interesting. Sierra and Liza weren't friends anymore. Sounds like Liza had made several enemies throughout her life, I thought, but replied, "I'm so happy for her. Give her my best when you talk to her."

"I certainly will. Enjoy those caramels!" Sally waved before heading into the back.

With my arms full of food and treats, Major and I finally made it home—at the exact same time Chase pulled into the driveway. He stepped out of his truck, looking exhausted but still managing a hungry smile when he saw the takeout bag from *Ringo's*.

"You read my mind, didn't you?"

I held up the bag of food. "Of course. Double cheeseburger, extra fries, and your favorite caramels."

His face lit up. "You're officially my favorite person."

"Figured as much," I teased, leading Major through the door and Chase followed. Once inside, I set the food on the counter and tossed Major a new plush bunny toy. "I think he's been missing the one at my place, so meet Bun-Bun 2.0."

Major pounced on it, tail wagging, before flopping onto the rug to happily nibble and whimper playfully at the toy.

Chase chuckled. "I think you just made his night."

We set up the large cushions in front of the fireplace, unwrapping our food as the fire crackled beside us. The warm glow of the flames made the room feel cozy, a welcome contrast to the chaos of the past few days.

"I've been thinking," I said between bites, "about the Harris family."

Chase raised an eyebrow. "Walter and Mabel?"

I nodded. "I overheard them at the hardware store. Something about a 'problem being taken care of.' It was cryptic, but it didn't sit right with me."

Chase chewed thoughtfully, then nodded. "They have a long family history in the community. But you know, they've been trying to buy up local properties for years. And if they saw Misty as an obstacle..."

"Exactly." I leaned forward. "What if they were trying to pressure her into selling the inn?"

Chase wiped his hands on a napkin. "It's a strong lead. I'll look into it first thing tomorrow."

I smiled, feeling a surge of satisfaction. "Good. Because Misty isn't the only suspect we should be looking at."

Chase tilted his head. "Speaking of suspects, have you been hanging out more with Gary than just your chowder date?"

I rolled my eyes. "Let me guess. April?" I asked, ignoring his question.

He tilted his head ever so slightly, a sly smile tugging at the corner of his mouth—as if he were quietly in on a secret. "Maybe."

"You're one to talk. You seem to be spending your evenings playing handyman for her."

Chase leaned back on his elbows, clearly amused. "Still jealous?"

"Please." I took a sip of my drink, then shrugged. "Besides, you should be the jealous one. Gary and I finally had lunch the other day."

He raised an eyebrow, looking me over with that complicated expression of his. "You know, I brought on our intermission, but that doesn't mean I like it." His voice dropped slightly. "And I've really missed you."

I swallowed, feeling a warmth that had nothing to do with the fire. "I've missed you, too. And for the record, our intermission was probably necessary. There's a lot we need to figure out still."

"Agreed."

For a moment, we just sat there, smothered by the hush of words we couldn't bring ourselves to say.

Finally, Chase exhaled and straightened his shoulders. "I've liked the time we've been spending together. I don't want to over-think this."

I nodded. "We don't have to."

We finished our meal in comfortable silence, letting the moment settle. Major, content with his new bunny, curled up between us, snoring softly. As the fire burned, I yawned, stretching my legs out. Chase chuckled. "You're fading on me, Scarlett."

"Long day," I murmured.

He hooked my leg with his. "Stay."

I didn't argue. Instead, I grabbed the blanket from the couch, draped it over us, and rested my head against his shoulder. The steady rise and fall of his breath, the warmth of the fire, and Major's sleepy grumbles made it impossible to keep my eyes open.

The last thing I heard before sleep took over was Chase's quiet whisper, "Goodnight, Scarlett, I'm glad you stayed."

Nine

The cool morning air bit at my cheeks as I kept pace beside Lily Johnson, the town's veterinarian and one of my closest friends. She matched my stride effortlessly, her brown ponytail bouncing with every step as we jogged past the *Sunflower Inn*.

"This festival gets bigger every year," Lily said between breaths, adjusting the sleeves of her sweatshirt.

I nodded. "More tourists, more vendors...and this time, a murder."

She grimaced. "Yeah. Misty must be a wreck."

"She is," I admitted. "She's convinced someone is trying to frame her."

Lily hesitated before speaking again. "You know, Vinnie was talking about Liza last night. Said he knew her family growing up."

That caught my attention. "Really?"

"Yeah. He said Liza was always...ruthless. Even as a kid, she had a habit of doing whatever it took to stay on top. But as she got older, it got worse. He's heard rumors over the years that she's been involved in some shady business deals. Nothing concrete, just whispers."

I frowned. "Interesting." Liza had made plenty of enemies. The question was, who hated her enough to kill her?

We veered onto the wooded trail behind Miller Park, where the festival crowd had yet to gather. Leaves crunched beneath our feet, and the faint scent of damp earth and pine surrounded us.

"I still can't believe someone poisoned her right at the festival," Lily said.

"Bold move," I agreed. "Risky, too."

As we neared the area where the crime scene had been the day before, still taped off due to the ongoing investigation, something caught my eye—a small glint of gold near the edge of the trail. I slowed my pace until I stopped.

"Hang on a sec," I said, crouching down, pretending to retie my shoe.

Using the cuff of my hoodie, I carefully scooped up the object and slipped it into my pocket. At first glance, it appeared to be a small button. I didn't dare pull it out for a closer look with Lily watching.

"Everything okay?" she asked, several paces ahead of me working on some hamstring stretches.

I forced a smile. "Yeah. Just needed to adjust my laces."

She nodded, and we continued our jog, but my mind was already racing. Had I just stumbled upon a new piece of evidence?

"You sure you're up for this?" Lily asked, casting me a sideways glance. "You seemed exhausted last night when I called to confirm our run."

I nodded. "I'm fine. Just fell asleep in front of the fire *again*."

Lily arched a brow. "Let me guess. With Chase?"

I shrugged, refusing to give her the satisfaction of seeing me blush. "Major was there, too."

She laughed. "Uh-huh. And the rumors about you and Gary?"

I groaned. "Please tell me people aren't actually talking about us."

"Oh, they're talking." Lily grinned, stretching her arms as we slowed near a bench. "Small town, Jules. You know how this works."

I rolled my eyes, deciding to change the subject. "Speaking of relationships, how are things with you and Vinnie?"

Lily's expression softened as she adjusted the sleeves of her sweatshirt. "Good. Really good, actually. He's sweet. Steady. The kind of guy you don't have to second-guess."

"Sounds nice." I bumped her arm with a light nudge, then winked. "Think he's the one?"

She hesitated for a moment before nodding. "We're not rushing into anything. Even though his divorce is final, Connie is still in the picture while they divide up their assets. But yeah, I do."

I smiled, genuinely happy for her. "I'm glad." We continued slowing to a cool-down pace. The trees rustled with the morning breeze, leaves tumbling down around us like golden confetti.

"So," Lily said, shifting gears. "What's your next move in the investigation?"

I sighed, kicking a stray acorn off the path. "I'm still looking at the Harris family. Walter and Mabel have been acting weird. I don't know them very well, but some of the things I overheard make me think they could be involved somehow."

Lily frowned. "You think they had something to do with Liza's murder?"

"I don't know yet, but I brought it up to Chase last night." I hesitated, then added, "When I overheard them talking at the hardware store, Walter was saying something about a 'problem being taken care of.' It was vague, but it didn't sit right with me."

Lily pursed her lips, thinking. "And what about Victor Langley? Gary stopped by to pick up some pet meds for his neighbor's cat. He's such a good guy. He kind of let it slip that you two overheard Victor at the festival. Then of course, he swore me to secrecy and I'm only mentioning it to you because you're like my best friend and you are sort of on the case."

I laughed. "Maybe you should tell Chase that. And yes, Victor was on the phone talking about Liza like she was a thorn in his side. We still need to figure out what business they had together."

Lily and I veered toward the bridge that crossed the park's small stream, the worn wooden planks creaking slightly beneath our feet. A few vendors were already trickling in, setting up booths or grabbing early morning coffee.

Lily adjusted her ponytail. "You know who I can't shake a bad feeling about? Ethan Harris."

I glanced at her in surprise. "Ethan?"

She shrugged. "I know he's been playing Misty's knight in shining armor for years, but something about him rubs me the wrong way. He's always there, always hovering. And he's way too eager to throw suspicion anywhere but at Misty."

I considered that. "You think he could be involved?"

"I wouldn't count him out. I think he wants to control the narrative," Lily said carefully. "Maybe he's protecting Misty. Maybe he's protecting himself."

A shiver ran down my spine. Maybe, he was protecting his parents. "I'll keep an eye on him." And made a mental note to mention that motive to Chase.

We stopped near the park's entrance, the festival officially coming to life around us. The sound of laughter and music filled the air, the scent of cinnamon rolls and cider stronger now.

Lily nudged me. "So, are you ever going to tell me what's actually going on between you and your men in uniform?"

I groaned. "Lily—"

"C'mon, seriously," she teased. "You can dodge the gossip all you want, but I know you and Chase have something real. I haven't quite figured out how Gary fits into this, but he's got an amazing character. Which leads me to ask, are you just being stubborn, or are they both actually that frustrating?"

I sighed, looking toward the festival where Chase was in the distance, talking to Liam, his newest deputy. "At this point I think I'm the frustrating one."

Lily giggled. "Sounds about right." She squeezed my arm before jogging away. "Good luck with the case, *detective*."

I shook my head, watching her go, then turned my attention back to the festival—and to the growing list of suspects that I needed to unravel. Not ready to deal with my reality, I headed home. The drama of my life could wait another day.

———

THE MORNING RUSH AT THE CAFÉ HAD JUST BEGUN TO slow when Gary strolled through the door, smells from my freshly brewed espresso blending wonderfully with the smell of his cologne as he approached.

"Detective," I greeted, raising an eyebrow as I wiped my hands on a towel. The rumor mill was about to explode with this very deliberate meet up, making me wish I'd headed straight to the festival instead of stopping here.

"Just a deputy," he corrected with a smile, resting his palms on the counter. "But if you want to call me detective, I won't argue."

I shook my head with a small, amused smile. "What brings you in? Don't tell me you're slacking off at work. The Sheriff will have your head."

Gary placed a five-dollar bill on the counter and leaned in slightly. "Your coffee is miles better than the stuff at the station."

I grinned. "That's because Chase is too cheap to buy organic beans."

Gary chuckled. "Roger that."

I poured a fresh cup, sliding it across the counter. "Anything new on the case?"

He took a sip, then shook his head. "Nothing solid yet. But I did want to check in on you."

I arched a brow. "On me? Why?"

Gary set down his cup, his expression softening. "I wanted you to know what I said at the park, I meant every word."

I swallowed. "Gary—"

He held up a hand. "Look, I know this thing with Chase is... not exactly straight forward. But I like you, Juli. Since the day you came back to town, I felt like we had a connection."

The sincerity in his voice caught me off guard. Without warning, he reached across the counter and took my hand in his. "Just think about it," he said, his thumb brushing lightly over my fingers. Before I could react, the front door burst open, my wooden chimes clanking around instead of creating their warm undertones.

"Juli!" Oliver stormed inside, Major trotting in beside him.

Gary pulled back, casually picking up his coffee as Oliver strode toward us, looking mildly exasperated.

"Chase dropped him off," Oliver said, nodding at Major. "Said Valerie's got the flu, you were...busy." He stopped to visibly scrutinize me and Gary before continuing, "So I was his next best option."

I blinked, surprised by his very obvious judgment. "And he just...dumped him on you?"

Oliver shrugged. "Basically."

Gary sipped his coffee, amused. "Guess Chase trusts you, then. He wouldn't hand Major over to just anyone."

Oliver shot him a pointed look. "Guess so."

Gary stood to leave. "Well, Juli, think about it." He winked, took his coffee and pastry, and walked out.

The scrutiny in Oliver's eyes continued as he turned to me, crossing his arms. "Care to explain what that was about?"

I sighed. There was no avoiding the question, and Oliver wasn't about to let this go.

He motioned toward an empty table in the back of the café, and I followed. He sat down, arms crossed once more, his expression smug. Major lay sprawled in a pool of sunshine, tail thumping loudly when Steve, my black and white café kitten, appeared and settled between his giant furry paws. Both were blissfully unaware of the brewing interrogation.

"So," Oliver started, stirring his coffee unnecessarily, "you and Deputy Maxwell. That was...interesting."

I grabbed a napkin and pointedly wiped non-existent crumbs off the table. "Not sure what you mean."

Oliver snorted. "Juli. He was holding your hand."

"Technically, he took my hand. Briefly."

Oliver grinned knowingly. "Uh-huh. And?"

"And nothing," I said, still avoiding his eyes.

"You gonna say yes to whatever invitation you're supposed to be thinking about?"

I sighed, crumbling the napkin and setting it aside. "I don't know."

Oliver leaned forward. "Because of Chase?"

My stomach twisted, the familiar ache of unresolved history settling in my chest. I had been back in New Hope for a while now. Long enough to know that Chase and I weren't just unfinished business. We were a sealed vault of dormant words and buried feelings. Things I was too afraid to face yet couldn't stop reaching for.

The truth was, I had spent the last decade telling myself I had moved on from him. That I was over the hurt, the betrayal. But maybe the real reason I couldn't take that next step—with Chase, Gary, or anyone else—was because I was afraid I never would be.

I swallowed hard, feeling the words rising in my throat. "Oliver..." I started, ready to finally confess out loud.

Oliver's phone buzzed violently on the table.

He grabbed it, frowning. "Misty?"

I watched his expression shift from concern to alarm.

"What?" He shot to his feet. "Are you okay? We're on our way." He hung up and looked at me. "Her owner's suite at the inn has been ransacked. Sheriff's already there."

I was already halfway through the café and reaching for my coat. "Let's go."

Ten

The *Sunflower Inn* was in chaos when we arrived.

The historic, white-washed brick exterior, softened by ivy climbing along the walls, usually made it feel like stepping back in time. The wraparound porch adorned with wooden rocking chairs and hanging baskets of bright yellow chrysanthemums still appeared grand even though it was flooded by spectators drawn to the scene by swirling patrol car lights.

The front door was slightly ajar. Inside, the scent of cinnamon lingered, though today, the usual warmth was overshadowed by tension. Misty stood in the main hallway, arms wrapped tightly around herself. Chase and Deputy Caldwell were near the staircase, notepads out, all business.

Oliver rushed to Misty's side. "What happened? Where's Ethan?" He scanned the lobby and surrounding areas for his adversary.

Misty rubbing her temples. "He convinced me to stay at his parents' place last night," she admitted. "Said I needed to get away from the stress."

Oliver's jaw twitched, but he forced a nod. "Right. Of course, he did."

"He'll be here soon," she added as if it were an afterthought.

I caught the flicker of irritation in Oliver's eyes. Ethan had been a little too eager to step into the role of Misty's protector, and Oliver clearly wasn't thrilled about it.

Chase, ever the professional, cleared his throat before addressing Misty. "Walk me through exactly what happened when you found your room ransacked."

"I came in early to grab my ledger and some other paperwork, and my suite was completely torn apart. Drawers dumped, pillows slashed, furniture moved... It looked like someone was looking for something specific."

Chase narrowed his eyes. "Was anything actually stolen?"

Misty hesitated, then shook her head. "No. That's the weird part. Nothing is missing. No money, no jewelry, not even my laptop."

"So, someone wasn't looking to steal," he murmured. Chase and I met each other's gaze, and in that shared moment, the answer unfolded between us—wordless, inevitable, and ours alone.

"They were searching," we said in unison.

Oliver planted his feet wide as he surveyed the scene. "For what?"

"That's what we need to figure out." Chase jotted something in his notebook before glancing at me. "Juli, I know what you're about to say—"

I placed my hands firmly at my waist. "I don't think you do."

"You're going to insist on helping. Again."

I lifted my chin. "You know I can be useful. We make a great team."

"No, we're not partners in this case."

"But—"

"Look," he said guiding me by my elbow away from everyone. "Our fireside brainstorming is one thing, but this? There are too many loose ends. We have no idea what we're dealing with yet. It could get dangerous."

I frowned but didn't argue. At least not out loud. If Chase wasn't ready to connect the dots, then I'd just have to do it myself.

Misty approached glancing about the room nervously. "What do we do now?"

Chase tucked his notes away. "You let me do my job. And you stay somewhere safe."

"Sheriff, I'm not leaving the inn. Sure, I did last night but maybe if I'd been here, they wouldn't have done this at all."

Oliver stepped forward, his face full of concern. "Or you could have gotten hurt."

"He's right," Chase agreed, then cast a pointed look at Oliver. "Make sure she's not alone until we figure this out."

Oliver nodded, his protective instincts kicking in. "I'm not going anywhere, Sheriff."

Misty sighed, and for the first time since we walked in, she appeared grateful. As Misty and Oliver walked away, I could feel the weight of everything Chase and I didn't say pressing between us.

There were still too many questions. Too many secrets. And I wasn't about to sit back and wait for someone else to answer them. We held a knowing stare before Major trotted up and pressed against Chase's leg, tail wagging. Chase bent to retrieve his leash and extended it in my direction.

I looked down, then up in confusion at the mischief practically glowing in his eyes. "I'm sorry, but what's this?"

Chase leveled a steady gaze at me. "You're in charge of him until Valerie's feeling better."

I raised an eyebrow. "I can't be a dog sitter right now. I have important things to do."

"Consider it a favor, since you're so determined to stay involved," he said, the corners of his mouth pulling into a slight smile. "Besides, you have prior experience, and he enjoys hanging out with you."

I narrowed my eyes and pressed my lips together. Truth be

told, since our 'intermission' I missed the giant rag mop. "Fine," I said, scratching behind Major's ears. "But I'm billing you in vegetarian takeout."

Chase shook his head, turned back to his notes, and signaled Liam. I'd obviously been dismissed.

Oliver appeared by my side, leaned near my ear and said in a low voice, "You're not actually going to stay out of it, are you?"

I flashed a devious grin. "Have I ever?"

He replied with a nod, "Good. Misty needs us."

"Us?" I felt my brows creep up to my hairline.

My train of thought was disrupted by the sudden commotion near the registration desk. We whipped our heads around to see people yelling and swatting their arms in the air. They ducked, dodged and ran for cover.

"What's going on?" Ollie ducked behind me out of reflex.

I stood tall, my eyes trained on the flurry of a blue and gold tornado.

"Scallywag."

———

THE PAIN IN THE BUTT PARROT HAD FLOWN THROUGH the open door and fluttered onto the bottom banister of the stairs. Cocking his head from side to side, he looked like a bird on a mission. The parrot's beady eyes flicked to the mess in the first-floor suite, then he let out a sharp squawk.

"Not supposed to know! Buried in the Stone!"

"Woof-Woof-Woof" Major tugged toward the bird.

"Juuuuli...click-click-click...half baked!" The crazy bird marched his taloned feet as if he'd given us the final piece of our murder puzzle.

I froze with a death grip on the leash.

Chase turned. "What did that bird just say?" He walked closer and Scallywag flapped his wings.

"It's the cops! Eeeeeek!"

"Woof-Woof-Woof!"

Before I could process what was happening, a second blur—this one furry and significantly larger—broke free from his leash and bounced after his feathered friend.

"Bad dog! Bad Juli!" Scallywag shrieked, wings flapping wildly as he flew over our heads.

"Major, no!" Chase's voice boomed, but it was no use. The sheepdog was already in full pursuit, knocking over a side table in his enthusiasm. A ceramic vase teetered dangerously before crashing to the floor in a spectacular explosion of colored porcelain.

Scallywag darted through the lobby, dive bombing patrons and Major. "She knows! She knows!" he squawked as he passed me.

I groaned. "Fantastic."

"You want to tell me what the bird is accusing you of now?" Chase drawled, dodging a toppled coat rack and trying to grab his dog.

"Sure," I snapped, lunging for the pesky parrot as he swooped over my head. "Let me just sit him down and have a chat. I'm sure he'd be more than happy to testify, Lawman."

Scallywag landed on the mantle. His beady black eyes gleamed with mischief. "She knows! Baaad Juli."

"He's ruining everything!" Misty cried as she and Oliver ran about the room. "Get him out of here!" She shooed at him with a fly swatter.

Chase leveled me with a look. "Well?"

I scowled and tossed my arms in the air. "How should I know what he's talking about?"

"Because he seems to think you do."

My jaw dropped. "And you're going to believe him?"

"It's payback time," Scallywag squawked as he launched himself from the mantle.

"Well, now he's just making stuff up." I hopped over an ottoman.

"Or," Chase mused, hands on hips trying to catch his breath, "he's mimicking something he actually heard."

"He's done it before." I shrugged.

Major, undeterred by our conversation, took another leap, jaws snapping at the air where Scallywag had just been. The parrot dodged and landed high in the chandelier, swinging in dizzying circles.

"I swear this bird is going to drive me insane," Misty muttered.

"I believe we passed insanity about five minutes ago," Oliver quipped from where he stood against the wall, a mix of amusement and exhaustion gleaming in his eyes.

Chase, however, wasn't amused. He moved closer, watching Scallywag with his investigative frown. "What exactly are we supposed to find?"

The frantic foul flapped his wings once more. "Bad Juuuli, she knows!"

The entire room fell silent.

I stared at the bird, a slow prickle of unease crept up my spine. "Chase," I said carefully, "if you're about to accuse me of something based on the ramblings of a rambunctious parrot, I swear—"

"I'm not accusing," Chase interrupted, his tone deceptively mild. "I'm just...curious."

Major, sensing the shift in mood, let out a huff and plopped onto the floor at Chase's feet, watching us like we were all crazy. To be fair, we probably were.

Misty sighed. "He must be repeating bits and pieces of things he's heard. It could be nothing."

"Or it could be something," Chase said pointedly. "Juli, if there's anything you want to share—"

"Oh, for crying out loud! I don't know what the bird is talking about." I stepped over the dog and moved toward Scallywag who flitted to a higher spot on a lamp. "If he's been feeding us cryptic clues, maybe we should be piecing them together and actually go look for something.”

Chase’s gaze narrowed. “What would you suggest?”

I straightened my shoulders. “I suggest that while you keep playing Sheriff Do-Good, I go looking for answers.”

His expression darkened. “Juli...”

“You said it yourself,” I pressed on. “Too many loose ends. Well, I’m going to tie some of them up.”

Scallywag cackled again, as if enjoying our little standoff. “Find it! Find it! Buried in stone! Nooobody knows!”

Chase let out a slow, measured breath. “Just don’t do anything stupid.”

I gave him my sweetest smile. “Who, me?”

“Juuuuli knows!” Scallywag shrieked before flying out the door.

I turned to follow, not looking back, heart pounding. Chase could protest all he wanted, but one thing was clear—Scallywag had just handed me a new lead. And I was going to find out exactly what it meant.

Eleven

The warm glow of *Coleman's Restaurant and Pub* was a sharp contrast to the cool October air. Inside, the murmur of conversation blended with the low hum of a football game playing on the TV behind the bar. I had followed Victor Langley from *Miller Park*, waiting for the right moment to strike up a conversation. He took a seat at the bar, ordered a scotch, and checked his phone.

I slid onto the stool next to him, ordering mulled cider. "Quite the crowd tonight," I said casually.

Langley barely glanced at me. "Festival weekend. Always good for business."

I turned slightly toward him, feigning polite curiosity. "I heard you had some business dealings with Liza Blake."

That got his attention. His mouth pressed into a firm line as he took a slow sip of his drink. "You could say that. Not that my business dealings are any of your business."

I raised an eyebrow. "I'm not prying into your business at all. I have a friend who was planning on working with her. Did you find her difficult to work with?"

Langley let out a low chuckle. "Difficult doesn't begin to cover it. Liza didn't just want in on my land investments—she wanted to call the shots in every way, if you get my drift." He swirled his drink before taking another sip. "She was relentless. A woman who always had an angle." He drained the glass and tapped the bar for another. "Not that it matters now."

I tilted my head, playing innocent. "What kind of investments are we talking about?"

Langley sighed, setting his glass down. "The same ones I've been trying to get Misty Shepard to consider for months. The *Sunflower Inn* sits on prime real estate—too much for one person to handle alone. I've been respectful, but she refuses to sell."

I kept my face neutral. "Misty loves that place. It's been in her family for generations."

"Of course she does." He gave me a knowing look. "But emotions don't keep a business afloat."

I leaned my elbow on the bar. "And if she did sell?"

His lips curled into a satisfied smirk. "Then I could finally move forward with my vacation cottages near *Miller Park*. I already have an office on the adjacent lot. Her property would complete the plan."

I forced a small smile. "Well, I wouldn't hold your breath. Misty isn't one to change her mind easily."

Langley sighed, finishing his drink. "That's what Liza said, too. And look where that got her."

Goosebumps danced over my skin. Was that just an observation? Or something more? I glanced down at my untouched cider, my mind already racing. One thing was clear—Liza wasn't the only obstacle in Langley's way. And now, Misty was next on that list.

I decided to push a little further. "You think someone killed Liza over business?"

Langley shrugged. "Wouldn't surprise me. She made enemies easily. If it wasn't me, it could've been someone else."

I studied him carefully. "Like who?"

He let out a low chuckle, swirling the last of his scotch in the glass. "Claire Bennett, for one. She had it out for Liza after losing that pie contest. A woman scorned, right?"

I bit the inside of my cheek. Claire's bitterness toward Misty had been evident, but toward Liza? That was new. "Claire's competitive, but that's a stretch."

"You don't know the half of it." He leaned in slightly and I could smell the alcohol on his breath. "Liza humiliated her. Told her she'd never amount to anything beyond second place." He scoffed. "If you ask me, Claire wanted to prove her wrong."

I filed that information away but didn't let it show on my face. Since Victor was freely giving information, I only paused for a breath before asking, "What about Walter and Mable Harris?"

Langley raised an eyebrow. "Now that's an interesting thought."

I played my suspicion casually, tracing a finger around the rim of my glass. "They've been worried about the inn for years. If Liza was working a deal with you, maybe she'd been playing them too and they wanted revenge." My mind raced with the blind theory that made sense once spoken out loud.

Langley let out a low chuckle. "You've got a sharp mind, Juli. But the Harrises are old money, and they don't get their hands dirty. They make problems disappear through paperwork and influence, not murder."

I wasn't so sure about that. "Still, if Misty's forced out, it could benefit them, too."

Langley stood, buttoning up his denim field coat. "Maybe. But if I were you, I'd look at who had the most to lose." He gave me a pointed glance before tossing a bill on the bar. "Good luck with that."

As he walked away, I sat there, my thoughts racing. Liza had enemies. More than I realized. But which one of them had been desperate or bold enough to kill her.

———

I stepped out of *Coleman's Pub*, pulling my coat tight as the night air settled over New Hope. I'd given Victor a fifteen-minute head start before leaving so as not to cause suspicion. He'd finished his second drink and excused himself, obviously done discussing Liza and his business with me. As I glanced up and down the street to make sure he wasn't going to follow me, I couldn't get his words out of my head.

That's what Liza said too. And look where that got her.

It could've been an off-hand remark. A generalization. But what if it wasn't? I walked briskly toward my truck, my mind spinning. Liza had been a problem for Victor—someone in his way. And if Misty ended up in prison for Liza's murder, her property would eventually go to an auction. Which meant Langley could swoop in, buy it for a fraction of its worth, and complete his future plans.

I needed to get home and revamp my suspect list.

I pressed the gas a little harder than usual, rushing back to the *Sunflower Inn*. Major greeted me with an excited bark, but I barely registered it as I clipped on his leash.

"Everything okay?" Oliver asked, coming from the dining area.

"It's all good." I held the leash tight and glanced toward the door. "You need a ride home or are you staying here tonight with Misty?"

"Ethan is here now." He glanced back toward the kitchen as we heard Misty's laughter. "She doesn't need me."

Before I could say anything, the swinging kitchen door burst open, and Misty emerged, still giggling as Ethan followed close behind her, an easy grin on his face. She swatted at his arm as if he'd just told her something hilarious. The moment she saw Oliver standing there, her smile faltered for a split second, but she recovered quickly.

"Oh! You're still here," Misty said, brushing a strand of hair behind her ear.

Oliver shoved his hands in his pockets. "Yeah. Just making sure you were okay."

Ethan draped an arm over Misty's shoulder, pulling her in slightly. "She's more than okay. I made sure of it." He grinned at Misty as if sharing a personal secret, then looked at Oliver. "I appreciate you being here earlier, man, but I've got things handled now."

Oliver stiffened, his easy demeanor slipping. "Sure."

Misty, oblivious to the tension settling between them, stood on her toes and kissed Ethan lightly on the cheek before stepping away. "I should get back to the kitchen. The last thing I need is Sandy Perkins telling me I abandoned my own business."

"Go," Ethan said warmly. "I'll be right here." Misty gave a small wave before disappearing back through the swinging door. Ethan turned his attention fully to Oliver, offering him a sly grin. "No hard feelings, right?"

Oliver's jaw tightened, but he forced a nod. "Right."

I glanced between them, and tension rolled off Oliver in waves. Ethan wasn't just thanking him; he was making a point. He had won—at least for now.

"Well," I said, trying to break the awkward silence, "I should get Major home and fed before he realizes he's hungry and terrorizes the kitchen staff." Oliver let out a breath, finally dragging his gaze to mine after Ethan walked away. "Oh, Ollie..." I placed my free hand on his shoulder. He looked like a lost puppy. "Remember what I said? They have a history she doesn't yet have with you."

"Just when I think she's giving me signs, he shows up and it's like I don't exist."

"Hmmm, kind of like someone else I know."

"Jules, you're confusing me."

"In other words, don't worry about it. When one door closes, another one opens. Just be patient." I couldn't let him in fully on Claire's feelings, just in case she ended up being the murderer.

"I suppose." He walked ahead a few steps. "Where have you been, anyway? I found the dog passed out by the fire."

"Having a conversation with Victor Langley. The plot thickens and I hope he's all talk and Misty isn't in danger."

"Danger!" His steps faltered. "Maybe I should stay here tonight."

"My gut says he's blowing smoke." I looped my arm through his, propelling forward once more. "Besides, Ethan won't let Langley through the door, let alone close enough to hurt Misty." I hated to say it, but it was true.

"You're right." Oliver shrugged. "Wanna stop and get Falafels?" Oliver said as he opened the door.

"Yes!" My stomach growled as if on cue. "Come on, big guy," I muttered to Major, leading him toward my pickup. "We've got work to do."

Twelve

The drive home was uneventful. Oliver jumped out of the truck, eagerly taking our dinner inside. The moment I stepped onto my front walk, Major stiffened. His ears flattened, and a low, rumbling growl started deep in his chest.

I stopped short. "What is it, Maj?"

A second later, a man stepped around the side of my house. He was well-dressed—a sleek black coat, polished shoes, expensive-looking watch. Everything about him screamed money.

"Can I help you?" I asked carefully, tightening my grip on Major's leash. The dog wasn't letting up. He barked and snarled, pulling forward like he wanted to lunge. The man barely reacted. Instead, he studied me with sharp eyes before speaking.

"My name is Rolf Müller. I'm looking for Oliver Thompson. I was told he was staying here."

The distant strains of music from the festival drifted though the early evening air, a stark contrast to the tension settling over my front yard. I was hyper-aware of the silence between me and this man.

"Who told you that?" I asked, stalling.

He smiled, but it didn't reach his eyes. "A friend."

I struggled to remember where I might have seen him before. His name wasn't familiar, but his face...something about it nagged at me.

I forced a casual stance. "Well, you were misinformed. Oliver doesn't live here."

Rolf cocked his head. "No?"

"Maybe you should check at the inn," I suggested, praying Oliver wouldn't decide to charge out the door to see what was taking me so long. "He's been helping Misty a lot lately."

Rolf's lips twitched at my lie. He stepped forward, lowering his voice. Major barked wildly, snapping at the air between us. "If you see him," Rolf said coolly, "tell him we need to talk. Soon."

"Who's 'we'?" I challenged, then blurted the first name that came to mind, "You and Eddie?" We hadn't heard about Eddie since he'd disappeared after the county fair. I'd hoped to never hear from him again. But I wouldn't put it past him to send someone back to New Hope if he felt there was something of value still here. Which could be Ollie's statue.

"Not Eddie," his eyes turned to slits, as if realizing I knew more than I was letting on. "Eddie doesn't have enough class to be in the same arena as my boss."

I swallowed hard. So, this was bigger than Eddie Costello.

That fact he knew who I was talking about sent a shiver up my spine in the worst possible way. While I should have been comforted that Rolf had nothing in common with Eddie, he apparently had a link to a different set of powerful people.

Rolf took another step forward, the air between us suddenly charged with implicit tension. "You're sure you don't know where he is?" His voice had turned silky smooth, but there was an underlying sharpness to it like the edge of a well-honed blade.

I held my ground, lifting my chin. "I told you, I don't know where he is."

Rolf's lips twisted into something sinister. "That's a shame. I'd hate for you to be caught in the middle of something you don't understand."

My stomach clenched as my worry meter came to life. "Is that a threat?"

His expression remained unreadable. "Why don't we call it a friendly warning."

"Juli!" A firm voice yelled, startling me from my intense focus. I spun around toward the sound. Chase's silhouette appeared massive against the glow of his indoor lights. He stepped onto his porch, his eyes immediately locking onto the tense situation. His expression darkened as he strode toward us.

"Something wrong here?" he asked, his tone dangerously even.

Rolf barely blinked. "Not at all. Just looking for an old friend."

Chase's stare was unwavering. "Funny. Doesn't look like she wants to chat."

Rolf took a deliberate step back, hands up in mock surrender. "Apologies. Didn't mean to cause any distress."

Chase crossed his arms. "That so? Because it sure looked like you were pressing her for something."

Rolf chuckled, shaking his head. "It's Sheriff, right? Are you always so quick to jump to conclusions?"

Chase didn't flinch. "It's my job to make sure people around here are safe. And right now, you don't look like someone who should be hanging around my town."

Rolf exhaled, feigning boredom. "I'll be out of here soon enough." Then he turned toward me, his cold expression returning. "But I do hope you pass along my message."

Chase took a step closer, his shoulders squared. "And if she doesn't?"

Rolf's gaze darted between the two of us, a glint of something dark passing through his expression. "Then I'll just have to find him myself."

He turned to leave, his polished shoes clicking against the sidewalk. Then, just as quickly as he appeared, he became swallowed by the growing shadows of the night.

Chase watched him go, his jaw tight. He didn't turn to me right away, instead following Rolf's retreating figure until he disappeared completely. Only then did he exhale sharply and look at me.

"You okay?"

I nodded, though my pulse was still racing. I'd wound Major's leash so tight my fingers were red. My worry meter clanged a five-alarm warning through my entire body. Rolf was bad news. The sooner I figured out who he was, the better for us all.

Chase's gaze flickered between me and the direction Rolf had gone. "What did he want?"

"Oliver." My voice came out steadier than I expected. "He said he was an old friend."

Chase scoffed. "Yeah, and I'm the Great and Powerful Oz."

I swallowed. "I told him Oliver wasn't here."

Chase studied me for a long beat. Then, with a sigh, he reached for Major's leash and gently pried it from my clenched fingers. "Come inside," Chase said, his voice soft but firm. "We need to talk."

I sent a quick text to Oliver, letting him know where I went. Then as I followed Chase up the steps to his porch, I stole one last glance over my shoulder, but Rolf was long gone. Yet, the uneasy weight in my chest remained. I had a terrible feeling that this was just the beginning. These were Oliver's Boston skeletons, not mine, and I knew I should have told Chase about this sooner.

CHASE'S RUSTIC LIVING ROOM FELT LIKE THE HUG I needed—comfortable and frustratingly familiar. I sat on the couch, lost in thought, my coat still on, hands buried in my pockets as I sifted through my mental index of contacts, trying to place where I knew Rolf from. Major plopped down by my feet, still on high alert. I couldn't blame him. My nerves vibrated like a plucked guitar string.

Chase poured two glasses of wine, handing me one before settling onto the couch beside me. I held up a small, tarnished key my fingers had been toying with inside the coat pocket.

"What's that?" he questioned while scrutinizing the key.

"I don't know how long it's been in Mom's pocket, or what it goes to. My dad used to have a small wooden box in the den he kept locked. I might check it tomorrow, if I remember. Either that or it goes to something from Mom's antique store."

"Maybe," Chase said quietly. "Or maybe it opens something you're better off leaving locked."

"What's that supposed to mean?" I shifted on the couch to face him.

He shrugged. "Some things are better left buried, Juli." He pointed toward his front door. "I have a feeling there's more to our current story. Wanna tell me what's going on?"

I took a slow sip before answering. "Rolf Müller. I told you, he was looking for Oliver."

Chase frowned. "And?"

I hesitated. I wasn't ready to tell him about Boston and Oliver's statue. Not yet. Not when Oliver had specifically asked that we figure this out together, on our own. But at the same time, keeping Chase in the dark felt wrong. He could help. He always helped. And yet, something about Rolf's presence made me feel like the fewer people involved, the safer we'd all be.

Instead, I deflected. "He said he was here for the festival. Claimed he was just 'catching up with an old friend.'"

Chase studied me. I could tell he didn't believe that for a second. His jaw tightened as he leaned forward, resting his elbows on his knees. "Juli, this guy wasn't just some random festivalgoer. He has you rattled. I see it all over your face. You gonna tell me why?"

I chewed my lower lip, then blew out a breath. "I don't know exactly. He just...felt off."

His brows pulled together. "There's something you're not telling me."

I looked away, focusing on Major as I idly stroked his fur. "Actually, I have a lot to catch you up on."

Chase cleared his throat, visibly frustrated, but giving me space to pivot. "Go on."

"I followed Victor Langley to *Coleman's Pub* tonight," I admitted.

"Juli..." He warned, his tone low, but he let me continue.

"He and Liza were involved—professionally and I even think personally. She wanted in on his land deals, but he found her too demanding. And he's been trying to buy the *Sunflower Inn* from Misty."

Chase dragged a hand down his face. "Gary already filled me in on the call you two overheard, remember?"

I nodded. "Yes, but this is the proof to the one-sided conversation we heard. What if Liza was the first obstacle? If Misty goes to prison, the land goes to auction. Langley could buy it for next to nothing. He could easily be the person framing Misty."

Chase's lips pressed into a thin line. "It's a theory."

"I also found what looks to be a button, and possibly a clue." This felt like the perfect time to let him in on my unofficial investigation skills.

"Where?" He leaned in, resting his forearms on his thighs.

"It's safely bagged in my office at the café," I said proudly.

Chase pinched the bridge of his nose. "No, I meant where did you find it?"

"In *Miller Park* when I was jogging a trail with Lily." I paused at his shocked expression. "Don't even say it, lawman, I've found an amazing stress reliever and just as amazing running buddy."

"Please, continue." He said, not even trying to hide his amusement.

"Whatever." I held up my palm as if to ward off his teasing. "Right after we'd jogged past Misty's booth, I caught sight of it along the edge of the path. I thought it might mean something."

"Hmmm, maybe, but I think it's a stretch. A lot of people use those trails, especially now with the added festival traffic and leaf peepers."

I shrugged. "Yeah, I guess."

The tension in the room was thick—not just about the case. About us.

We were both trying. Trying to be normal. Trying not to let the past creep in. But it was there, lurking beneath every glance, every pause, every sip of wine. My pulse pounded as I worked up the courage to tell him more—to tell him about Oliver, the statue, Boston—when a sharp knock sounded at the door.

Chase cursed under his breath and stood. He set down his drink and I watched him walk to the door, frustration rolling off him in waves. Our conversation wasn't finished, and he didn't like that anymore than I did.

When he opened the door, my heart sank.

There, stood April Henderson.

She was dressed for dinner—a trendy khaki trench coat, hair perfectly curled, lips painted a deep red. "Hey," she greeted with a smile, nonchalantly standing on tiptoe to kiss his cheek as if it were an everyday occurrence. "You ready?"

Chase rubbed the back of his neck. "Yeah. Give me a second."

Her gaze drifted past him to me, and I saw her smile tighten.

"Juli," she said smoothly.

"April."

Unvoiced thoughts lingered in the charged silence between us. Chase, oblivious or maybe just ignoring it, muttered something about changing his shirt and disappeared down the hall. April stepped inside, closing the door behind her. She folded her hands in front of her waist and studied me, a slow smile playing on her lips.

"So, you and Chase," she mused, her voice dripping with something I didn't have the brainpower to identify in the moment. "Still playing this little will-we-won't-we game?

I stiffened. "I'm not sure what you mean."

She tilted her head, fully engaged. "C'mon, Juli. We all see it. And honestly, I think it's sweet. In a tragic sort of way. Maybe it's time to accept that Chase wants to move on."

The words landed like a punch to my gut, but I kept my expression neutral. "Is that what he told you?"

She laughed softly, "He doesn't have to. Actions speak louder than words, don't they?"

Chase reappeared, fresh shirt on and hair slightly mussed from running a hand through it. He glanced between us, sensing the shift in the air. I had a mind to call her out right in front of him, just to see how he'd respond, but I refrained.

"Everything good?" he asked, breaking into my thoughts.

April flashed a bright smile. "Of course. Ready to go? We have reservations in Port Byron, and we can't be late."

Chase hesitated, like maybe he felt guilty, and my heart skipped a beat. "Juli, can you feed Major and lock up?"

I managed a fleeting smile, hoping he didn't see my discomfort. "Sure."

He turned back to April, took her by the hand and said, "Let's go."

As the door shut behind them, I let out a pent-up breath. Major whined at my feet, nudging my hand. I scratched behind his fluffy ears. "Yeah, boy," I murmured. "That makes two of us."

Thirteen

"*Tap-Tap-Tap. Tap taptap tap. Tap-Tap-Tap.*"

Major whined.

"*Tap-Tap-Tap. Taptaptaptaptaptaptap. Tap-Tap.*"

I'd barely slept thanks to my overactive imagination which had flipped all night long between *who the heck Rolf Müller was* and *what the heck were Chase and April doing*. At some point, Chase had let the dog into my house and Major had found his way to the foot of my bed—only to have us both startled awake by Scallywag tapping on my window.

So much for my snuggle buddy. He bolted to the window, and I rushed to toss on a pair of leggings and a sweatshirt. Moments later, we were out the door.

"Scallywag, you naughty bird, get back here!" I ground out between my clenched teeth as I ran down my front porch with Major in tow.

The swift sweep of the bird's massive colorful wings skimmed the street like a living brushstroke in flight, cackling as he led Major and me on a wild chase through town. The parrot had somehow escaped from Mrs. Bailey's house again, and Major—taking his self-assigned job as "bird wrangler" very seriously—broke free of his leash and tore after him.

"Major!" I groaned, stumbling forward as the leash slipped from my hands. "You are a working dog, not a bird dog!"

"Woof-Woof"

The chase led us straight toward the *Sunflower Inn*. Scallywag plunged toward the chimney, taunting Major with a loud, "Bad Dog! Bad Juli!" before diving toward the grassy courtyard. Major lunged, leaping just high enough in the air to catch Scallywag's tail feathers in his mouth. Scallywag screeched like a teenage girl. I wouldn't be surprised if someone had dialed 9-1-1.

"Major, drop it!"

The dog obeyed immediately, releasing the parrot, who squawked and flopped onto the grass in a dramatic heap. I rolled my eyes. "Did Mrs. B send you to birdie acting school?" I snapped, jabbing my hands at my waist. "C'mon, Scally. You're fine."

Scallywag gave a couple weak squeaks, hopping toward the chimney, noticeably flapping one wing and for a moment I wondered if he'd really been injured. That is, until he stretched his massive wings, bobbed his head a few times and began pecking aggressively at the stone. Major, now wildly interested and not to be outdone, barked, pawing at the bricks, and whined.

"What are you two doing? Misty doesn't need any more repairs to make." Stepping closer, I ran my hand along the brick Scallywag had been drawn to. "We're trying to help the inn, not cause more problems."

"Juli?"

I turned just as Oliver jogged toward me, his brows drawn in confusion. His gray hoodie wasn't even pulled down over his t-shirt. He looked like he'd just rolled out of bed with his brown hair stuck up on one side. "I heard you yelling... Why are you chasing that parrot through town at—" he checked his watch, "—seven in the morning?"

"Because Major is a bad influence," I grumbled, nodding

toward the smug-looking sheepdog now sniffing at the chimney. "And I'm too sleep-deprived to be making good choices."

Oliver released a quiet laugh, but his expression shifted when he saw the way Major was pawing at the bricks. Scallywag, apparently over his feigned injury, flapped onto Oliver's shoulder and gave an excited, "Click-click-click."

"Looks like you've got a new friend," I said, then stepped closer to inspect what had them so worked up. This time there was an uneven edge of a loose brick, and I frowned. "That's weird…" I said under my breath.

"Let me see." Ollie crouched beside me. He jiggled the white-washed brick and gave it a firm tug. It gave way with a sharp crack, revealing a hollow space behind it.

My breath caught when I saw what was nestled inside—a small, journal. I swallowed hard and reached for it, my heart pounding. I flipped open the cover and my breath whooshed out. "Liza Blake," I whispered, and looked at Oliver, my jaw slack.

He leaned over. "That's her journal?"

I nodded, gripping the leather-bound book tighter. "It has her name inside."

Silence stretched between us, the weight of the discovery anchoring us in place. Scallywag made more clicking noises and flapped into the air to land on Major's back. "Gooood Dog," he cooed while he perched there like they were suddenly the best of friends.

"Great," I said. "I don't know how I feel about the two of you being partners in crime."

"Okay," Oliver released on a big breath. "What's going on with you?"

"Why don't you start by telling me what's going on with you?" I stood, brushing the grass from my knees.

He shrugged and said, "Well, for starters I'm pretty sure Misty isn't interested."

"I'm not talking about Misty, Ollie." I held his stare for a moment. "Someone named Rolf Müller was looking for you."

"Yeah, I saw him through the window." Oliver pulled at the hem of his hoodie.

"Something tells me that if you only had the nerve, you'd actually be able to face him."

"Funny, Jules, very funny." He shot me a look conveying his displeasure. But this was Oliver, and I could tell him anything, and I was just getting started.

"Mind telling me what he's doing in New Hope?"

His jaw tensed. "What did he say?"

"That he was here for the festival...but we both know that's a lie." I lowered my voice. "Chase stepped in before I could get much out of him, so what does he want with you?"

Oliver swore under his breath, running a hand through his shaggy hair. "Damn, Jules."

Guilt twisted in my gut. "I should've told Chase," I admitted. "But I was trying to keep my word to you."

Oliver sighed. "I appreciate that."

"Do you think he's behind the mysterious note you received at the inn?"

"It would seem about right." Oliver sighed and leaned against the washed-out bricks of the chimney stack. "I think he's here about my statue."

"Why not just ask you to give it back? Why resort to scare tactics?" I shivered when I remembered Rolf's mention of his boss. "Who does he work for?"

"I don't know." He shook his head. "Maybe we're in over our heads."

I nodded slowly as I thought about the things Rolf had said. "Yeah. Maybe we are."

Movement caught my eye. I glanced up to see Claire walking down the sidewalk, her hands tucked into the pockets of her coat. An idea sparked.

"Oliver," I said quickly, nodding toward the street, "Go talk to Claire."

He frowned. "What? Why?"

"Because I need time to look through this." I held up the journal. "And because she likes you."

"Excuse me?" His eyes widened.

I leaned against the bricks beside him, hugging Liza's journal to my chest. "Claire told me she has feelings for you, but she thinks you're still hung up on Misty."

Oliver opened his mouth, then closed it. "What if Claire is the one framing Misty?"

"She might not be," I countered, still not sure if Claire played a role in Liza's murder but maybe this journal would have the answer. "And maybe it's time you let Misty go. Focus on someone who actually cares about you."

He paused, his gaze darting from me to Claire. Slowly, his shoulders drooped. "You really think so?" he asked quietly.

"Yes, I do."

Something shifted in his expression—like maybe, just maybe, he was considering it. Taking a deep breath, he straightened and started toward Claire. "Hey!" he called, flagging her down. She turned, surprised, and then smiled. Within moments, they were walking together in the direction of the café.

Exhaling shakily, I watched them go, relieved to be alone. "Okay, Liza," I murmured while glancing down at the journal. "Let's see what you were hiding."

BY THE TIME I GOT HOME, MY MENAGERIE HAD settled into their respective places. I dropped Scallywag back into his cage at Mrs. Bailey's, ignoring his indignant screeching, then took Major to my back deck. The night air was cool, the sky streaked with the glow of the setting sun. I curled into one of the cushioned chairs, flipping open Liza's journal.

At first, it was just names, figures, and scribbled notes—random pieces of what looked like business dealings or even leads. But as I turned the pages, my breath caught. Liza had written:
Walter and Mabel Harris.

- *Approached me about edging Misty out of business.*
- *They want the Sunflower Inn back in their family.*
- *They are willing to back me in whatever I have to do to make it happen.*

I inhaled sharply, my suspicions now confirmed. But there was something else. Two words, like a name, had been written and then erased. I couldn't make it out on the paper. I scanned the passage again, my stomach twisting. This wasn't just about the Harrises. Liza had dirt on someone else. Someone who might have had just as much to lose.

Did they know about this notebook? Is that why the name was taken out? If so, then I might have just put myself in serious danger.

A sharp knock on my back gate made me jump. My pulse spiked as I snapped the journal shut, glancing over my shoulder toward the dim yard. Major, who had been lounging beside me, let out a low, lazy woof but didn't move from his spot. Not a threat, then.

I stood and peered through the slats of the fence. Oliver's familiar shape stood on the other side, hands in his pockets. His hair was slightly neater than before, but he still had that just-rolled-out-of-bed look about him.

I opened the gate. "Back so soon?"

He grinned and stepped inside, his eyes bright with something I hadn't seen in a long time—hope. "Claire and I are going to the festival together. There's a new comedian on stage at the gazebo.

And I might be cooking dinner at her place later. So don't wait up."

I blinked. "Wow. That's...fast."

He shrugged, but there was a lightness to his posture. "We just had coffee, and we talked. A lot. She admitted she had been jealous, but she realized she needed to be happy for me, no matter what I chose." He ran a hand through his hair. "I believe her, Jules. She's the most genuine person I've ever met. I don't believe Claire's framing Misty."

I studied him, watching the way his face softened at Claire's name. This wasn't like the Oliver I'd seen chasing after Misty, always chasing something just out of reach. This was different.

I smiled. "I'm happy for you, Ollie. Really."

He gave me a long look, then nodded. "Thanks." He gestured toward the journal still clutched in my hand. "What about you? What have you found so far?"

I hesitated. Sharing this with Oliver felt different than telling Chase or even Gary. Oliver knew things—about Boston, about me—that no one else did.

Sighing, I motioned for him to sit. "You're not going to like it."

He dropped onto the chair beside me, leaning in as I flipped the journal open again. I showed him the page with Walter and Mabel Harris's names, watching his expression darken as he read.

"Damn," he muttered. "I knew they wanted the inn back, but this..." He trailed off, rubbing a hand over his jaw. "Backing her in whatever she had to do? That's pretty incriminating."

"I know." I chewed on my lower lip. "But look at this." I pointed to the faint smudge of erased words. "Someone else's name was here, Oliver."

"How do you know it just wasn't a doodle or something?"

"I don't, but I think it's an honest conclusion that Liza wasn't a nice person. What if she was up to something and someone found out about it?"

He exhaled. "Do you think that's why she was killed?"

I nodded slowly. "I think it's very possible. Liza had a reputation. She could have made a bad deal or upset the wrong person."

"Wouldn't our favorite sheriff call that speculation?"

"Look who's being a comedian now," I scoffed. "I prefer to call it coffee-fueled crime solving with a side of creative genius. What if Liza had proof of something—something big—then whoever this was could have found out. Maybe they thought she'd double-crossed them. Maybe they wanted to silence her before she could."

Oliver sat back, arms crossed. "Are you going to tell Chase?"

I sat quiet for a moment. "Not yet."

His brows lifted. "Jules, you know how the sheriff feels about rules and such."

"I know. I just…" I closed my eyes and breathed through the struggle, knowing I couldn't get this wrong. "This is still too vague. We don't know what, exactly was erased. If it even was someone's name, or maybe it's a place. And if I bring this to Chase now, he'll push for answers I don't have and dismiss my ideas."

Oliver studied me, then nodded. "I get it. You don't want to jump the gun."

"Exactly." I ran my fingers over the page. "I need to figure out what was erased. If I can do that, then maybe I'll have enough to take to Chase."

Oliver leaned forward, elbows on his knees. "So, what's the plan?"

I glanced at the faint marks again, my brain churning. "Well, I could try to get the imprint of what was written before it was erased. Sometimes, if you lightly shade over it with a pencil, you can see the indentations."

Oliver arched a brow. "That actually works?"

"Sometimes." I stood and went inside, grabbing a pencil from my kitchen drawer. When I returned, Oliver had pulled the small patio table closer and turned on the flashlight on his phone. I carefully laid the journal flat, angling it so the light hit the page at just the right slant. Then, I took the side of the pencil's lead and gently rubbed it over the paper. Slowly, faint letters began to emerge.

Oliver sucked in a breath. "Holy—"

"Shh," I whispered, my heart thudding. More letters appeared, forming part of a name. My stomach twisted as I read them aloud.

"It looks like an 'l' and a 'y'."

Oliver leaned closer. "You think it's Langley? Ugh, I wish more letters would show up. Maybe you need to rub harder, Nancy Drew."

"I don't think it works that way, and I don't want to ruin it. Langley makes sense. Liza was looking into land deals. Langley has been trying to expand his properties for years. Maybe she found something shady about his deals, and he got spooked, or angry."

Oliver tapped his fingers on the table. "Langley has deep pockets, Jules. If he wanted to make something disappear—including a person—he has the means to do it."

A jolt of unease gripped me. "Yeah. And I might be holding the evidence that could prove it."

Oliver frowned. "You need to be careful."

"I know."

He stood and gave me a quick hug. "Look, I should get going. Claire's waiting, and I promised I wouldn't be late."

I stared at him in surprise. "You? Punctual? Who are you?"

He laughed, shaking his head. "Apparently, someone who actually wants to impress a girl for once."

I walked him to the gate, watching as he disappeared down the street. When I turned back, Major was staring at me with those deep, knowing eyes.

"You think I should tell Chase, don't you?" I asked the dog.

He wagged his tail once.

I sighed. "Yeah. I know."

But I wasn't ready. Not yet. I needed more. And if Langley really was involved, I needed to be sure before I accidentally put myself in danger.

Fourteen

After being chased inside by mosquitos, I curled up on my couch, picking at a fruit and cheese platter, my appetite practically nonexistent. Across the room, Liza's notebook was tucked under a cushion, hidden but burning a hole in my conscience. I wasn't ready to share it. Not yet. I needed proof that Liza's accusations were true before I pointed fingers at the wrong person.

The sound of Chase's truck pulling up outside sent my heart into a strange, uneasy rhythm. Major, sprawled beside me, lifted his head and thumped his tail, excited to see his owner. After three quick knocks, the front door swung open. Chase stepped inside, his uniform slightly rumpled, jaw tight, eyes sharp.

He was obviously troubled.

"Glad you're still up," he said, his voice edged with frustration when he stopped in front of me. "You want to tell me why Rolf Müller is really in town?"

I popped a grape into my mouth, stalling. "I told you—he was looking for Oliver."

Chase folded his arms. "And I told you my gut says he's connected to Boston."

I swallowed hard. "I don't know that for sure."

His eyes narrowed. "Stop this. Don't play dumb when we both know you're anything but."

I set my plate down, sighing. "Chase, I'm not keeping secrets—"

His laugh was sharp and humorless. "Really? Because I've gnawed on this all day, and it feels exactly like all the other times you've kept something from me."

I winced, thinking of the journal. "Look," I said, lacing my fingers together. "I was going to tell you, but I needed to be sure first."

Chase paced, running a hand through his hair, then stopped before me. "That's your excuse every time, Juli. You 'needed to be sure.'" He air quoted. "You 'didn't want to make assumptions.' Meanwhile, I'm standing here like a damn fool, waiting for you to trust me enough to let me in."

Guilt twisted in my stomach. "I just—"

"Just what?" He shook his head, his voice softened a bit. "You promised me, Juli. No more waiting until it's convenient for you to tell me the truth. No more Boston skeletons. And I believe you. I believed you!" He tossed his hands in the air.

I pressed my lips together, feeling the guilt squeezing me from the inside out. "Rolf works for someone who I think might be connected to the gallery," I admitted, my voice quieter now. "I don't know who. But it's not Eddie, David, or the Percy brothers."

Chase released a deep breath through his nose, shaking his head. "So, you did know something."

"Yes!" I shot to my feet, the force of my own voice surprising me. "But I only just found out. I wasn't trying to keep it from you —I was trying to piece things together!" My words came in a rush, desperate to bridge the gap stretching between us.

His laugh was cold and sharp like broken glass. "Of course you were." His voice tightened, the tone slicing through me. "Because that's what you do, isn't it? Figure things out by yourself, always by yourself."

I opened my mouth, a rebuttal forming, but his next words struck like thunder.

"You never let me in, Juli," he said, his voice breaking under the strain. "You keep me at arm's length, like I'm a damn safety net. You pull me close when it suits you, but you're too scared—too stubborn—to let me stay."

The rawness in his voice cracked something open inside me and I couldn't stop myself from blurting out, "Because the one time I needed someone to stay, he walked away without another word." I paused as unspoken pain hitched within my chest. "I think you know more about why my father left home than you've ever admitted."

His expression changed. For the briefest second, I saw something there—regret, maybe. Or guilt. But just as quickly, it was gone.

"That's what this is about? No, you can't pin that on me. You walked out on us just like your father walked out on you and your mom."

"Chase, that's not fair."

"What about now?" He let out a bitter, humorless laugh that scraped against my nerves causing me to shiver. "It's like you're shoving me toward April."

"April?" I scoffed, the pressure in my chest almost unbearable. "That's ridiculous! You're doing that all on your own. Or you're letting her do it."

His eyes, blazing between anger and anguish, pinned me in place. "You think this is a joke?" His voice dropped low, but the intensity only grew. "You act like it's some foregone conclusion, that I'm destined to be with April because you—" He stepped closer, his words trembling under the weight of emotion. "Because you won't let me get close enough."

I couldn't move, couldn't breathe. Every word carved its way into me, leaving nothing untouched.

"And you know what's worse?" His voice cracked, just once, but it shattered everything. "I've told you, Juli, over and over again. I've never wanted her the way I've wanted you. But I guess that's not enough for you. I'm not enough."

The air between us seemed to vanish, and I could do nothing but stand there, his confession echoing in the silence like a storm about to break.

"Maybe if you were honest with me," the words escaped in soft breaths before I could catch them, "about what you really know, about why my dad left. Maybe then, I wouldn't second-guess myself every time I want to trust you."

Chase flinched just enough that I saw it. His jaw clenched. His gaze, which had met mine with such conviction seconds ago, faltered for the first time. He didn't look away—not yet—but his voice was quieter when he spoke. "Juli...it's not what you think."

"Then what is it?" I asked. "Because you've known something for years, and you've never told me. You always want to know why I left, yet you won't be honest with me." I stared at him, feeling the well of tears. "How can I be honest with you?"

He shifted his weight, like the ground under him had tilted. "What your father did—what happened—it wasn't just about your family" he shook his head slowly, his voice thick with something I couldn't name and had never heard from him before. "If I told you, you'd look at a lot of people in this town differently. Maybe even me."

The words knocked the breath out of me. "What are you saying?"

He didn't answer. Maybe he couldn't. Chase took a slow step back, ran a hand over his mouth like he was trying to hold something in. Then, finally, he looked away. A pause stretched between us, and when he spoke again, his voice was tight, distant. "I can't do this anymore"

His words sank like stones into the pit of my stomach, and I stumbled forward, desperate to close the widening chasm between us. "Chase—"

"You got what you wanted," he cut in, a sad, almost resigned smile ghosting across his lips. "A clean break." He turned, the slump of his shoulders carrying the gravity of his words.

"No! That's not—" My hand shot out instinctively, but I froze mid-step as he turned back to face me. His gaze—hollow, yet piercing—stopped me cold.

"The funny thing is..." His voice cracked faintly, a thread unravelling. "I keep letting you do this. Over and over. So maybe this mess is just as much my fault as it is yours." He shook his head, a bitter laugh catching in his throat. "But I always thought...somehow, some way...we could beat the odds."

"I used to think so, too, you know."

His eyes met mine. "Then what happened?"

I swallowed hard. My fingers itched to reach for his, but I stayed perfectly still, my voice low when I spoke, "I convinced myself my father left because something was wrong with me."

Chase blinked. "How so?"

"Come on, I was sixteen," I went on. "You know how rebellious I was. Always sneaking out, breaking curfew. I thought if I stopped complaining about working at the antique shop, helped Mom more at home...he'd come back." I gave a short, humorless laugh. "It's stupid, I know. I just wanted to make sense of something that never will."

Chase didn't say anything. Didn't move.

"And there you were," I said, even quieter now, "always steady, always there. And I thought...at least someone stayed."

A long silence followed, heavy enough to press against my chest. Broken only by the sorrow woven into each word as he spoke, "Yet you chose to leave."

He reached into his coat pocket and pulled out the napkin I'd given him—a simple, crumpled token. "I've spent all day trying to understand this. Why it means nothing to you...and why it still means everything to me." His hand trembled as he pressed the napkin into mine, the paper crinkling between my fingers.

"Chase." It was all I could manage, a whispered plea buried in the rising tide of tears.

He raised his now empty hand, halting whatever useless explanation I had bubbling up inside me. "Not this time, Scarlett." The nickname stung, pulling memories of my younger self to the surface. Memories where I had been reckless, thoughtless, and so convinced I could fix everything on my own. I swallowed them down as he took a deep breath to speak. "I love you enough to let you go."

And I knew, then, what he meant. I knew what I'd done—not just now, but long before this moment.

An eternity passed as Chase Hargrave stared into the depths of my crumbling soul, his final goodbye etched into the silence. He turned toward the door and whistled for Major, who scrambled to his feet, though he hesitated between us, his big brown eyes searching for direction.

"Let's go," Chase ordered softly, his voice steady but distant. Major whimpered and nudged my hand, his warm nose a fleeting comfort against my skin.

"Not this time, big guy," I whispered, brushing my hand over his fluffy back. "Go on." My voice cracked as the words escaped, the crushing significance of the moment settled into my bones, unyielding and unforgiving.

And then they were gone.

I stood there, clutching the napkin to my chest like a talisman against the ache ripping through me, staring into the void of their absence. The truth of everything—of *us*—tumbled over me like a rogue wave, and all I could do was let it drown me.

———

THE NEXT COUPLE OF DAYS I BURIED MYSELF IN LIZA'S journal, anything to keep my mind from spiraling. Chase's words echoed in my head, but I shoved them aside, focusing on the pages in front of me. Page after page, Liza had written down everything —names, figures, and notes. But when I hit the section about Walter and Mabel Harris, my breath caught. Beyond her bullet points were details of a conversation I couldn't believe.

Walter and Mabel advised they have a plan already in place as a security measure to get the Sunflower Inn. Foolish of them to confide in me. I could ruin them in a heartbeat. Maybe it's time to get all the old money out of this town. Bring in new blood and new businesses. Plan on bringing this to Victor's attention over dinner and dessert...

I skimmed the undated pages until another entry caught my attention.

The fact that I can ruin Sierra's life from across the country gives me such joy! An old friend checked into my B&B and happened to fill me in on her 'fresh start' with some athletics company. She has no idea how far my network extends. I vowed I'd make her pay for humiliating me all those years ago. She's never learned her lesson. She'd better watch herself or I'll ruin this relationship like I did the last one. I'm going to call it my SWEET Revenge!

Eager to learn more I flipped through the pages.

Unexpected meeting this morning. She knows! She's already threatened me and caused a potential investor to back out of a deal. I'm done playing nice. There's a rat in New Hope and I have a good idea where to start. S.F.I.

"Is she talking about the *Sunflower Inn*?" I questioned out loud.

My fingers tightened around the journal. Liza hadn't just been stirring the pot. She had ended up being the real target. I sat back, my chest tightening. Liza had been about to do something—something big. And someone had made sure she never got the chance. How did this involve the inn?

I needed answers. And I had a feeling Claire Bennett was a good place to start.

I tucked the journal safely within my bookshelf. As I was grabbing my coat, there was a knock on the door. I peeked through the curtain and relaxed.

There stood Gary with a smile and a bouquet of flowers.

"Gary? What are you doing here?"

"I ran into Oliver at the café, and he told me what happened with you and Chase. I just wanted to see if you were okay and bring you some flowers to cheer you up." He extended his hand containing beautiful fall blooms.

"I'm okay. You know, keeping busy on the case so I don't have to think about my failed relationships."

"Were you going out?" He nodded toward the coat draped over my arm. My first instinct was to be truthful and say yes, but I hadn't formulated a plan yet as far as Claire was concerned. I couldn't count on Chase to run through the suspects, but maybe Gary would. Why tell Chase about the journal when I could tell Gary. He was far less complicated, and right now, that was what I needed.

"You know, why don't you come in? Do you have time?"

"Of course!" he eagerly replied, and I opened the door wider for him to pass through. Gary stepped inside, his sharp eyes immediately scanning the room as if piecing things together before I even said a word. That was something I appreciated about him, he was always paying attention, always listening. And unlike Chase, he didn't doubt me. He never had.

I led him to the kitchen table, pulling out the chair across from mine and gesturing for him to sit. He did, setting the bouquet carefully on the counter before turning his full attention to me. "So," he said, leaning forward, elbows on the table. "What's going on?"

I hesitated for a beat, putting the flowers in water as I gathered my thoughts. I had trusted Chase with my theories before, but I always felt like I was trying to prove myself to him, like I had to work twice as hard to be taken seriously. Gary didn't judge me or poke holes in my theories. He believed in me. And after everything that had happened, he was the only person I wanted to confide in.

I grabbed the journal from the bookshelf and set it between us. "This is Liza Blake's journal. I found it hidden behind a brick at the *Sunflower Inn*."

Gary's eyebrows lifted. "Hidden?"

"In the outside chimney stack." I tapped the cover. "She documented everything—conversations, plans, names. And she erased one of them."

Gary reached for the journal, flipping it open to the page I had been obsessing over. He studied the faint smudge where Liza had erased something, his expression turning thoughtful. "She erased a name?"

I nodded. "I used a pencil to shade over it and got part of it back—only an 'l' and 'y'. I think it could be Victor Langley."

His eyes darkened. "Could be. That guy's been trying to get his hands on half the town for years."

"Exactly. And if Liza had something on him, something that made him nervous enough to have her silenced..." I let the sentence hang in the air.

Gary ran a hand over his chin, then nodded. "That makes sense. But you might be able to get more of the erased letters back. We have to be sure before we go around interrogating people or arresting them with no justification."

I perked up. "How?"

"Oblique lighting."

I frowned. "What's that?"

He leaned back, folding his arms. "If you shine a light at an angle across the paper, sometimes the indentations from the erased words become more visible. It works better than just shading over it with a pencil."

I sat up straighter. "That's brilliant."

Gary flashed a self-assured grin. "I do have my moments."

I rolled my eyes, but I was already thinking ahead. "Any ideas on how to do it?"

Gary tapped the table, thinking. "April might be able to help. I'm sure her photography studio has all kinds of specialized lighting equipment. Ultraviolet light is another method. She could get the right angle and maybe even enhance it digitally."

My stomach twisted at the mention of April. "No."

Gary frowned. "No?"

I forced a casual shrug, but my voice betrayed me. "I just... don't want to bother her."

His gaze softened. "Juli."

I let out a sharp breath. "Chase is moving forward with her. I don't need to go knocking on her door asking for favors, or anything...ever."

Gary watched me for a moment before nodding. "Okay. Then we figure something else out."

His simple acceptance surprised me. He wasn't pushing, wasn't telling me to let it go or to 'be happy for them.' He was just...here. On my side. I swallowed past the lump in my throat. "Thanks, Gary."

He smiled. "Always."

I cleared my throat and redirected my focus. "Okay, so let's talk theories. If Langley was involved, that means money was involved. Maybe Liza found something illegal—fraud, bribery—something big enough to make him nervous."

Gary nodded. "And if Langley's name was erased, maybe there were other names, too. Businessmen like him, have other contacts, they don't necessarily work alone."

"Exactly. We need to figure out what would make Liza hide her journal in the chimney stack at the inn."

"Or who," Gary added, unknowingly fueling my fire.

I flipped back to another entry and pointed. "Like here. She mentioned ruining Sierra's life from across the country. Sally told me Sierra and Liza had a falling out, but she didn't go into details. Who else but Liza had that kind of reach? She mentioned her network, what does that even mean? This is New Hope, small town America."

Gary studied the passage, then looked at me. "What if the person Liza erased wasn't just an accomplice? What if they were the real mastermind, Sierra Sweet is collateral damage and Langley was just another player?"

Unease crept slowly down my spine. "Then we might be chasing the wrong person."

Gary nodded. "Which means we need to dig deeper. And fast."

"I've got some questions for Claire about Oliver. Maybe I'll see if she knows anything about Sierra Sweet."

"Great," Gary replied, his amber eyes flashing with newfound excitement. "I'm going to touch base with the Harrises. Maybe I can get them to fill me in on any secrets they might know about Liza."

I took a deep breath and met his gaze. "Perfect. Then let's do it."

Fifteen

Ringo's Diner was comfortably packed for a late-morning lull, the scent of fresh coffee mingling with fried bacon and the buttery aroma of pancakes from a late brunch order. The hum of conversation and the occasional clink of silverware filled the room. Behind the counter, Vinnie leaned against the register, listening intently to my best friend Lily, his girlfriend, as she recounted a story about her cat knocking over a lamp at her veterinary office. A couple of retirees occupied the counter seats, nursing cups of coffee while chatting about an upcoming historical society meeting.

Claire sat near the window, a ceramic mug curled between her fingers. Wisps of steam barely rose above the rim as her tea cooled. I slid into the seat across from her and she straightened, her eyes wary.

"Juli?"

"Sorry to bother you, but I saw you as I was passing by and had to come in. I need to ask you something," I said, my voice even, though my mind was already piecing together potential outcomes of this conversation.

Claire hesitated before setting her mug down. "Okay…"

I laced my fingers together on the table and leaned forward slightly, lowering my voice. "Your resentment toward Misty—it's not really all about Oliver, is it?"

I flagged Scott Iverson who was busy training his brother, Kyle, on the ins and outs of working at the diner. Within seconds he was bringing me a cup of coffee. "Cream only, just how you like it."

"Thanks Scott." I smiled. "Don't forget you're closing today with Andie."

"I know. Kyle is done in another hour. I'll have plenty of time." He left as quickly as he came, on to the next waiting customer, with his brother paying close attention.

She exhaled, long and slow, and placed her spoon on the napkin beside her plate. "It's not as dramatic as you think."

I lifted an eyebrow. "Try me."

She hesitated again, her gaze shifting to the half-eaten piece of lemon cake on the plate between us. Finally, she spoke. "Oliver met me for coffee a few days ago."

"Oliver told me how he feels about you. I'm wondering what you think about him?" I was very protective of my best friend. I could tell he was smitten with Claire, and it was miles apart from how he reacted when he first met Misty.

"He told me he likes me." Her voice was steady, but I detected something measured in her tone, as if she were trying to gauge my reaction. "But he wants to see where things go with Misty first before making any decisions."

I studied her carefully. "And you're okay with that?"

She nodded. "I like Oliver. But I think...he's going to realize sooner or later that Misty and Ethan have unfinished business."

I considered her response, searching for any flicker of dishonesty. But Claire remained open, sincere. If Oliver had truly seen something worth pursuing, it wasn't out of manipulation or competition—it was real. And that meant Claire wasn't trying to push Misty out of the picture to gain the upper hand. She actually thought enough of him to wait.

I sat back and blew out a slow breath.

Claire offered a small smile, as if she knew what I was thinking. "I know what I want, Juli. Oliver needs to figure out what he wants before either of us gets hurt."

I couldn't argue with her logic. Oliver had the biggest heart of anyone I knew, but he could also be very impulsive. I found myself full of respect for Claire and her point-blank approach to what was happening. My mind quickly veered back to the bigger issue at hand. I cleared my throat before diving in. "I have to ask...what do you think of Ethan?"

Her brows furrowed. "What about him?"

"You believe he and Misty are rekindling something. Is it possible Ethan killed Liza for Misty's sake? To protect her or get her out from under Liza's threats?"

Claire mulled over the question, tapping a finger against her mug. "Ethan has always been protective of Misty, but a killer?" She frowned. "I can't see him taking it that far."

"What about Misty?" I pressed. "Could she have done it to get Liza off her back?"

Claire's mouth tightened. "I'd like to think Misty wouldn't do something so drastic, but I don't know. She never handled threats well, and she and Liza had history." Her expression shifted, more thoughtful than surprised. "You don't think so, do you?"

I shook my head, remembering the shocked expression on Misty's face when Liza started choking and gagging. "No. She seemed genuinely fearful of how incriminating Liza's death was to her. I think she's been too overwhelmed with the inn to be that calculating."

I sighed, glancing toward the counter where Vinnie now exchanged knowing glances with a regular who was clearly spinning a tale he'd heard before. The easygoing atmosphere of the diner felt at odds with the tension bubbling in my chest.

"Do you know anything about Sierra Sweet?" I asked suddenly. "Since you've remained in town all these years, did you ever hear of Sierra and Liza having a fight?"

Claire looked confused. "Sierra Sweet? I don't remember hearing anything about a fight."

I frowned. Liza had seemed vindictive in her journal, as if she had dirt on Sierra from across the country. If Claire had no recollection, then maybe Liza had been holding onto something Sierra didn't even know about.

My mind raced with possibilities, but I forced myself to focus. "All right," I said, finishing off the rest of my coffee. "Thanks for answering my questions. I'm just looking out for Oliver's feelings."

Claire gave me a wary glance. "Sounded to me like you are trying to solve Liza's murder. Shouldn't you be leaving that to the Sheriff and his team?"

I stood, gathering my coat. "I always leave the official business to New Hope's finest. Don't worry, you have nothing to worry about."

She shook her head, jaw slack. "I'm not worried. I was just jealous, and I'm not anymore."

I smiled as I shrugged, then turned toward the exit. As I pushed through the glass door, the crisp autumn air greeted me, cooling the thoughts running rampant in my head. I firmly believed we could cross Claire off our suspect list. All she wanted was a chance with Oliver. She was no threat to Misty and had no reason to kill Liza. Ethan was still too protective of Misty for my liking, which made me think there was something else going on with him. I wasn't sure that had to do with Liza either. With too many pieces still missing, I needed to meet up with Gary and see how his conversation with the Harrises had gone.

I pulled out my phone and shot him a text. **Meet me at the café. I think we're onto something.**

As I walked toward my truck, the pieces of the puzzle shifted in my mind. Whoever had killed Liza had done so to silence her.

And I was getting closer to finding out why. One thing became clearer by the second. Misty didn't kill Liza. If Misty and Claire were both innocent...

That meant the real killer was still out there.

———

THE SOOTHING TONES OF THE WOODEN CHIMES ABOVE the door felt like home as I stepped into my café, the comforting scent of coffee and freshly baked pumpkin scones wrapping around me like a warm embrace. Gary was already seated at a corner table, a mischievous smile playing on his lips as he waved me over.

"I took the liberty of ordering for us," he said as I slid into the chair across from him. "Grilled cheese panini and fries," he said, indicating the food on the table, already waiting. "I figured you wouldn't turn down your own food."

I smiled, shaking my head. "You would be right."

He rested his forearms on the table. "I try."

A current of energy passed between us, but I shoved it aside. We had work to do.

"So, what did you find out about Walt and Mabel Harris?" I asked, reaching for my iced tea. "Are they looking guilty, or are we barking up the wrong tree?"

Gary rubbed his jaw. "Guilty of wanting the inn? Absolutely. But murder? I'm not so sure."

I frowned. "What did they say?"

"They came clean about their plan," he said, leaning back against the chair. "Get this, turns out, their goal all along was to get Ethan to marry Misty so the *Sunflower Inn* would be back in their family."

I blinked, pausing, the fry just inches from my lips. "Wait. What?"

"Yeah, you heard me." He shook his head, amused. "Apparently, generations ago, the Harris family owned the inn. That is, until one of them lost it in a poker game to a Shepard."

I let out a low whistle. "That must sting."

"You have no idea. They've been trying to get it back ever since. Ethan agreed to help them, said he'd been working on Misty for years, but she wasn't interested. When it became clear that a romance wasn't happening, Walt and Mabel realized they needed another way."

I narrowed my eyes. "Which is where Liza came in."

Gary nodded. "Bingo. They asked for her help in nudging Misty out of the business. But when Liza refused, they knew they had to find another way to acquire the inn."

I tapped my fingers against the table, mulling it over. "That's a solid motive for wanting Liza gone. But did they actually kill her?"

"That's the thing." Gary dragged his fry through a puddle of ketchup. "They said they wouldn't be stupid enough to take out someone like Liza when she knew so much about their other business interests. If anything, they were afraid of what she might do to them."

That gave me pause. "Interesting. So, if they didn't kill her, who did?"

Gary sighed. "That's the million-dollar question."

I picked at my panini, my thoughts swirling. "I talked to Claire about Sierra Sweet. She had no recollection of any fight between them, which means that lead might be dead in the water unless we can track down someone else who knew about it."

Gary nodded. "I can dig into that. Maybe see if I can track down one of Liza's other sources. Someone had to know about her history with Sierra."

"That would help." I took a bite of my sandwich, chewing thoughtfully. "In the meantime, I'm going to go through Liza's journal again. See if there's anything I missed. Someone or something has to connect all of this."

Gary grinned. "You know, working this case together is kind of exciting."

I arched an eyebrow. "Oh yeah?"

"Yeah." He nudged his plate aside and folded his hands. "And maybe...it's the beginning of us spending more time together."

I hesitated, caught off guard by his honesty. "Gary, I—"

He held up a hand. "I know, I know. Everything with Chase is still raw. And I respect that. But I've enjoyed this. And I think you have, too."

I sighed, swirling the lemon slice around in my tea. "I won't lie. I have. But right now, we need to focus on making sure Misty and Claire remain innocent. And most importantly, finding the real killer."

Gary nodded, his expression understanding. "Fair enough."

We finished our meal in comfortable silence, both lost in thought.

As I stood to leave, Gary reached for my hand, stopping me. "Juli, be careful, okay? If Liza was killed because she knew too much, you might be putting yourself in danger."

I met his gaze, a small shiver running down my spine. "I know. But that's a risk I have to take."

He squeezed my hand briefly before letting go. "Then at least don't take it alone."

I gave him a small smile before heading out into the cool autumn air. As I walked toward my truck, something gnawed at the edges of my mind. There was still a missing piece to this puzzle. Something I was overlooking.

And I had a feeling that whatever it was...it was about to change everything.

Sixteen

The fire hall smelled like burnt coffee, rubber, and fuel with a touch of smoke. The kind of scent that clung to small-town meeting spaces like it had soaked into the walls decades ago. Fluorescent lights flickered overhead, casting a harsh glow over the rows of metal folding chairs that had just been pushed aside. Now, with the Historical Society meeting officially over, the real reason Gary had dragged me here was about to begin—social hour.

People clustered in small groups, chatting over plates of homemade snickerdoodles and Styrofoam cups of cider that Betty Henderson was ladling out like it contained the secret to eternal life. From the way her husband, Harry, was holding his cup and grimacing after each sip, I had my doubts about what she'd spiked it with.

"This is exactly why I wanted to come," Gary murmured, leaning in so close that I could feel the warmth of his breath against my ear. "People loosen up when there's sugar involved."

I fought back a grin, taking a sip of my own drink. "Good thing you didn't bring a notebook. They'd clam up the second they saw you in full deputy mode."

He pressed a hand to his chest in mock offense. "You wound me, Butler. I can be incredibly subtle, you know."

I arched an eyebrow at him. "You asked Betty Henderson three minutes ago if she knew of any 'mysterious town secrets,' and she immediately started talking about the old postmaster's affair."

Gary grinned. "Well, that's good gossip. But not the kind we're after."

He scanned the room, then nodded toward a small group gathered in the corner. Mrs. Bailey stood at the center of it, chatting with Mayor Hannah Montgomery, Harry and Betty Henderson, and Sandy and Bill Perkins. If there was anyone in town who knew about the *Sunflower Inn's* history, it was our beloved Mrs. Bailey.

We made our way over, and I plastered on a friendly smile. "Evening, Mrs. B. I enjoyed your presentation earlier."

She gave a small, pleased nod. "Oh, thank you, dear. Though I imagine it was more thrilling for those of us who remember when the town archives were kept in my basement rather than a proper office."

Gary chuckled. "That must have been a treasure trove." He shifted slightly, his tone casual but his intent clear. "Actually, Juli and I were hoping to pick your brain about something."

Mrs. Bailey straightened a little, her sharp eyes locking onto him. "Oh?"

"The *Sunflower Inn*," he said. "We were wondering if you knew anything about its original ownership. If there are any restrictions on what can be done with the property."

At the mention of the inn, the small group perked up.

"What about it?" Bill Perkins asked, folding his arms across his chest.

Gary kept his voice light, but I could see the calculation in his eyes. "We heard rumors that there were plans to...change its ownership. We're just trying to get a sense of its history."

Mrs. Bailey's expression softened into something closer to amusement. "Of course, I know about the inn. I've been the

Historical Society's records keeper for over thirty years." She folded her hands over her purse and gave us a look like we should have known better than to ask. "The *Sunflower Inn* is a protected historical landmark. Has been for decades. It can't be torn down or altered."

I blinked. "Are you sure?"

"Absolutely," she said. "It was designated over thirty-five years ago, and the Society has funds earmarked for its maintenance and restoration. There's still money left in the budget that could go toward renovations if needed."

I turned to Gary, my heart racing. "That means Misty never needed outside investors or a loan. I wonder if she even knows about the budget money?"

"Her parents knew, of course," Mrs. Bailey added.

Gary nodded, his brow furrowed. "And they wouldn't necessarily tell her unless she made them aware of repairs."

"Because some of us are capable of doing things on our own," I interjected.

"Which means," he continued, "that whoever was trying to take the inn from her had other motives."

Sandy Perkins stepped forward with a frown. "Wait—what exactly is going on with the inn?"

I hesitated, but Mrs. Bailey's sharp gaze pinned me in place. "Something's not right, is it my dear?"

I glanced at Gary, weighing how much to say. Finally, I settled on a half-truth. "We're just trying to make sense of a few things. This helps. A lot."

Gary gave Mrs. Bailey one of his signature grins. "I have a feeling Misty doesn't know about the earmarked funds. You might have just saved the *Sunflower Inn*."

Mrs. Bailey huffed, but there was warmth in her expression. "Our beloved inn was never in any real danger—not legally. But it sounds like you two might know more than you're letting on."

The thrill of the chase settled deep in my chest, a familiar excitement buzzing under my skin. We were close—closer than ever. And despite everything else, I couldn't ignore how much I was enjoying it.

"We do. As soon as we have everything together, we'll share. Right now, we have more work to do."

Beside me, Gary leaned in as we walked away, his voice low. "I have to say, solving a mystery with you is kind of fun."

I grinned. "Don't get used to it."

"Too late."

We stepped outside into the crisp night air, the hum of conversation still trailing from behind us. The streetlights cast a gentle glow on the cracked pavement, and I paused near the front steps of the fire hall.

"You know," I said, "when you first suggested coming here, I thought you just wanted an excuse to eat cookies and hear about the old postmaster's secret love life."

"I mean," Gary said nudging me with his elbow, "that was part of it. But getting confirmation about the inn? Now that's a win."

A gust of wind stirred the leaves along the curb, and for a moment, I let a rare calm settle in. "It sure is. And I think Misty finally gets to breathe easy."

Gary looked at me, his expression a mix of warmth and admiration. "So do you."

We stood there a second longer, the night quiet except for the faint sound of someone's distant laughter. Whatever tomorrow brought, I knew we'd face it as a team.

———

THE NEXT MORNING, I PUSHED OPEN THE DOOR TO *Petite Four Paws Café*, expecting to find Mark behind the counter prepping for the afternoon rush, but instead, I walked straight into the last person I expected to see—Chase.

I stopped short, my breath catching in my throat. He was just stepping away from the counter, a to-go tray in one hand and a small bakery bag in the other. His uniform was crisp, his badge glinting under the warm café lights, and his dark hair curled slightly at the ends, as if he'd just run a towel through it after taking a quick shower. For a brief moment, his gaze flicked up, and something unreadable crossed his face before his usual cool expression settled in.

Seeing him here, so unexpectedly, was like stepping into a memory I wasn't ready to revisit. A part of me, treacherous and unguarded, longed to reach for the familiarity we used to share. But the tighter grip on the past only seemed to make the ache of our lost relationship sharper.

"Didn't expect to see you here," I said, forcing my voice to sound casual as I stepped aside so the door could swing shut behind me.

Chase held up the tray, which had two large coffees balanced on top. "Liam and I have concert duty at *Miller Park*. Thought I'd start the day off on a good note." He lifted the bakery bag slightly. "For Major. Figured I owed him."

I glanced at the bag and immediately recognized the signature packaging of the blueberry yogurt bones that we stocked just for the regulars with canine companions. Major's favorites. I swallowed against the warmth rising in my chest, unwilling to let the soft spot I had for Chase—and his dog—get the best of me.

"He still mad at you for working too much?" I asked lightly, hoping the humor would smooth over the awkwardness closing in.

Chase smiled, but the edge in his expression didn't quite disappear. "Oh yeah. Won't even sit next to me on the couch. Liam said I needed to make nice before he stages a full mutiny."

I couldn't help it. My lips twitched with the shadow of a smile. Chase had always been good at making serious things seem lighter, but even his attempt at humor couldn't hide the tension we shared simmering beneath the surface.

I nodded toward the counter and started to move past him. "Mark around?"

"Just stepped out," he replied. And then, before I could brush past, he added, "I'm still looking into Rolf Müller."

I paused, glancing back at him. "And?"

He let out a quiet sigh, shifting his weight. "So far, nothing concrete. No records in town, no connections to anyone local. It's like he doesn't exist."

My stomach churned as I folded my arms. "That's impossible. No one's a ghost."

"I know," Chase said, his tone serious, his brow furrowing as his gaze locked onto mine. "But he's sure as hell trying to look like one. He's been keeping a pretty low profile in town. I haven't seen him since that night outside your house."

Frustration clawed at me, but I wasn't surprised. This case was full of missing pieces, and every time I thought I had a lead, it slipped through my fingers.

Chase's gaze lingered on me, careful and unreadable, before he finally spoke. "What's wrong?"

The question disarmed me, slipping through the cracks in my resolve. I thought about brushing it off, burying it under something lighter. But his eyes—steady, searching—compelled me to be honest. "I don't know," I said softly, "I feel like we're getting closer to something, but it's still...out of reach."

He nodded slowly, his jaw clenching for just a beat before he spoke. "I'm not giving up. We'll figure it out." The words, while simple, carried weight—carried a steadiness that reminded me of all the times I'd leaned on him without even realizing it. Despite the distance, despite the fractured pieces, something still held us tethered.

The air around us seemed too heavy, and I cleared my throat, suddenly needing space. "You should get going," I said, glancing at the coffees still in his hand. "Wouldn't want Major to think you forgot about him."

Chase gave a subtle nod, a flicker of something unreadable crossing his face before the expression faltered as if caught on the edge of something deeper. He stepped toward the door, but before pushing it open, he hesitated. His hand brushed the doorframe, his back stiffening, and for a split second, his gaze darted back to me.

"See you around, Scarlett," he said quietly, the nickname slipping out as naturally as ever. Then, a spark of awareness passed across his face—a brief tightening of his lips, as if he'd suddenly remembered where things stood between us. And yet, he let the name stand, the undeniable intimacy of it hanging in the air as he walked out.

I stood rooted in place, staring at the closed door, the faint scent of coffee and something bittersweet lingering behind him. That moment—when he called me by the name only he used—hit me harder than I expected. It wasn't just a nickname. It was a reminder of what we had been...and what we weren't anymore.

Seventeen

The low hum of conversation and clatter from the kitchen filled *Ringo's Diner*, the only place in town where you could get a decent burger and catch up on all the town gossip depending on which booth you were sitting in.

Claire Bennett had agreed to meet with Chase to discuss Liza, but she had asked Oliver to meet her here for moral support. Oliver, being Oliver, immediately looped me in as well. "You two are a great crime-solving team," he said before dragging me through the door. Oliver and I had claimed a booth near the back, away from most of the noise. When Claire arrived, she slid in next to Oliver, leaving Chase to claim the spot next to me once he showed up.

Now, as Chase flipped open his notebook, pen poised, I noticed the way his shoulders were set—distant, professional, all business. The air between us still carried the same unspoken tension from earlier at the café, but I pushed it aside. This was about Liza.

Chase got right to it. "Claire, I need you to think back. Liza seemed to have her hand in a lot of things. Do you remember anything about her past dealings? Any names that came up frequently? Friends she relied on?"

Claire hesitated, twirling the straw in her soda, shifting uncomfortably under his sharp gaze. "Liza was...private. Even when I worked for her at the bed and breakfast, she didn't talk about personal things much. She had connections everywhere, but I wouldn't call them 'friends' exactly. More like people she could use when she needed something."

Oliver let out a low whistle. "Sounds about right from what little I observed of the woman."

I studied Claire's face. She looked nervous, like she wanted to say more but was holding back. "What about people from out of town?" I pressed.

Claire paused, tapping her finger to her lips. "You know, after thinking about our last conversation, I do remember Liza having some kind of interaction with Sierra Sweet."

Chase's eyebrows shot up. "You two talked about Liza?" His voice was level, but there was a subtle edge to his tone that made my stomach flip. His gaze snapped to me, his brow raised in disbelief. "When were you going to mention that?"

"I—" My words tangled in my throat. "It didn't seem relevant at the time."

"Not buying it." Chase leaned forward, his forearms resting on the table. "Considering everything we've been trying to piece together, I think anything about Liza qualifies as relevant."

Oliver raised a hand like he was flagging down a waiter. "Anyone else feel the tension in here or just me?"

"Not helping," I muttered, glaring at him briefly before turning back to Chase. "Look, it was nothing. At the time, she didn't have any dirt on Liza. But what she did do is basically give me reason to let Ethan and Misty off the hook as possible suspects."

"And you didn't think that was worth bringing up? Like

maybe my guys and I were wasting resources?" Chase pressed, his tone softening but still tinged with frustration.

"Can we not do this right now, Deputy Do-Good?" I said, trying to stay calm under his gaze. "I didn't realize it was a big deal."

"It's Sheriff, and anything about *my* case is a big deal, until I say it isn't," he said, his eyes narrowing slightly. "You don't know what might be important, Juli."

Claire cleared her throat pointedly. "For what it's worth, Chase, Juli wasn't wrong to bring Liza up with me. It helped jog my memory a bit as far as Sierra goes. But honestly, that girl is all the way on the West Coast now, so I don't know how anything about her would play into Liza's murder. Besides, whenever anyone talks about Sierra Sweet, not a bad word is ever said."

The tension in Chase's shoulders eased, but the intensity of his stare lingered. "We'll talk about this later," he said firmly in my direction as he leaned back in the booth.

I let out a slow and easy breath. As awkward as it felt in the beginning, the fleeting moments of how we used to be helped make working together possible. We could get through this professionally.

"I do remember their relationship always seemed to be strained," Claire added on a rush.

Chase and I snapped our heads toward each other, then toward Claire.

"What?" we both said.

"Liza and Sierra." Claire's confused features stared at us as if we were crazy.

"Of course! Strained how?" I interjected before Chase could move on to his next question. The thought Sierra could somehow be involved kept nagging at my gut.

"One disagreement after another. I never knew why, but the few times I took a message for Liza, Sierra always seemed angry. I'd heard they had once been friends but had a falling out. I really don't understand why they'd stay in touch at all." She settled her gaze on Chase. "You might want to get a contact number and ask her yourself, if you think it's worth digging into."

Chase jotted something down, then glanced up. "Anything else stand out? Even small things can matter."

Claire bit her lip. "Liza did have a few people she liked to gossip with. She was always talking to Vinnie Minetti. But that was mostly small talk—at least, as far as I know. I think she was interested in one of his brothers or something."

Chase tapped his pen against the table. "Noted." He sat up straight, the tension in his shoulders loosening just slightly. "I think that's enough for now." He snapped the notebook shut. "I need a sea salt caramel fix if I'm going to keep my focus on this case."

Oliver grinned. "You know, that's the first human thing you've said all day."

Chase raised an eyebrow but didn't argue as he slid out of the booth. Claire followed, brushing a strand of hair behind her ear. "I hope this was helpful, Chase."

His tone remained neutral, "I'll let you know if I need anything else." His gaze shifted to mine and for a moment I thought he would say more. Instead, he pursed his lips together before giving me a short nod and walking away.

Before Claire left, she turned to Oliver. "Dinner tomorrow?"

Oliver's whole face brightened. "Wouldn't miss it."

I raised my eyebrows but didn't comment. As Claire walked out, the gears in my brain turned. Something about this conversation had triggered a memory. Then, it hit me.

The purple ribbon.

I had found it tucked inside Liza's journal, marking a page. A detail I had skimmed over at the time, but now? It felt important somehow.

"Oliver," I said suddenly, standing up so fast my knees hit the table. "We need to get back to the house."

Oliver blinked. "Whoa, what? What just happened? Did I miss something?"

I grabbed my coat. "I think I just found our next clue."

———

OLIVER AND I RACED INTO MY HOUSE, WHERE THE scent of my vanilla-teakwood candle lingered from my morning meditation. I barely took off my coat before heading straight to the kitchen table, where I had left my bag with Liza's journal inside.

Oliver followed, looking amused but intrigued. "Are you going to tell me what we're looking for, or is this one of those times where I just stand here until you have a lightbulb moment?"

I ignored him, pulling out the worn leather journal and flipping through the pages with urgency. I stopped when I reached the pale purple lace ribbon. It had been tucked between the pages so neatly, marking a specific entry.

"Right here. The ribbon." My breath hitched as I looked at the page it marked. It was decorated with floral stickers and tiny hearts, and written in the center in Liza's sharp handwriting were the words:

"Doug will always be mine."

I stared at it. "Doug?" I muttered. "Who the heck is Doug?"

Oliver leaned over my shoulder, reading it for himself. "That's...weirdly personal for someone who was all about documenting their devious deals and contacts. And, extremely ambiguous."

I traced my fingers over the ink. "You're right, it doesn't fit. Liza was strategic. Calculating. Why would she put something like this in a journal filled with business dealings?"

Oliver took a step back, his expression thoughtful. "Maybe because whoever Doug is, he was important to her. Important enough to mark it with that ribbon."

My stomach churned. "Which means he might be connected to her death."

Oliver rubbed his hands together. "We need to find out who Doug is."

I nodded slowly, my mind racing. "And thanks to Claire, I think I know who might have some answers."

Oliver raised a brow. "Don't keep me in suspense."

I closed the journal and met his gaze. "Vinnie Minetti."

Oliver blinked, then let out a low chuckle. "Of course. Based on what you've told me about New Hope, the guy's been flipping pancakes and collecting town gossip for decades. If anyone knew the real Liza, it's him."

The importance of my discovery settled in my chest. This was the first solid lead we had in a while, and something told me that "Doug" was a piece of the puzzle we hadn't even realized was missing.

"We should talk to Vinnie first thing tomorrow," I said.

Oliver nodded. "Agreed. But for now? You need to eat something. You've been running on coffee and determination for days."

I sighed, rubbing my temple. "Yeah, yeah."

Despite the exhaustion creeping in, I felt it. That undeniable spark. We were finally getting somewhere. And for the first time in days, I had the feeling that we were on the verge of something monumental.

I just wasn't sure if we were ready for the truth to be revealed.

Eighteen

The morning breeze carried the scent of pine and the faint sweetness of autumn leaves as Lily and I set off down the trail. The sun had barely crested over the trees, casting long shadows across the damp earth. The rhythmic sound of our sneakers against the dirt path mixed with the distant crow of a rooster waking up the town.

Dew clung to the grass lining the trail, glinting faintly in the sunlight. The towering trees overhead created a canopy, their leaves tinged with orange and gold, rustling softly with each gust of wind. A chipmunk darted across the path ahead and into the safety of a hollowed-out log. The woods felt alive, yet peaceful, a stark contrast to the turmoil swirling inside me.

Lily had convinced me to go for a jog with her, claiming I needed to "clear my head," but I had a sneaking suspicion she had ulterior motives. She always did.

"So," she said, matching my stride as we weaved through the winding trail. "What's going on with the case? And don't try to dodge the question. I have the stamina to keep this up all morning."

I let out a slow breath, choosing my words carefully. "We

found a name in Liza's journal. Someone named Doug. We're trying to figure out who he is and what he meant to her."

Lily nodded, but I could see the gleam in her eyes that told me she wasn't just here for case details. "And what about local law enforcement? More specifically, Chase? You two have been dancing around something for a while."

I focused on the path ahead. "This isn't about Chase."

"Oh, come on, Jules," she huffed. "I know you'd rather talk town secrets than your love life, but you can't fool me. You've got all sorts of emotions bouncing off your aura. Sorry, but you can't hide those kinds of secrets."

I exhaled sharply, my breath forming a small cloud in the chilly air. "Fine. You know Chase and I are over. Well...Gary is making a move."

Lily nearly tripped over a rock. "Wait, Gary as in Officer Bland-but-handsome Gary?"

"The very one."

"And?"

"And nothing. It wasn't some grand moment. He was subtle. I was caught off guard, and then I told him I needed to focus on the case."

Lily gave me a look that screamed you're impossible, but thankfully, she let it drop. "Okay, back to the case then. What do you need?"

I slowed my pace. "I need to talk to Vinnie about Liza's past. Think he'd be willing?"

Lily didn't hesitate. "Absolutely. He loves to reminisce. If Liza had dirt, Vinnie probably knows where it's buried."

As we approached the edge of the trail, the town's early morning rhythm began to spill into the air. The faint hum of cars on the main road grew louder, mingling with the distant sound of a dog barking. With that, we turned off the trail and made our way toward *Ringo's Diner*.

The scent of waffles and fresh coffee welcomed me the

moment we stepped inside. The diner had its usual morning crowd —locals sipping coffee, reading newspapers, and chatting town gossip. Sunlight streamed through the wide windows, casting warm golden beams across the red retro booths. The soft hum of a jukebox in the corner filled the space with a comforting tune from the past, blending seamlessly with the steady clang of plates and pans from the kitchen.

Vinnie Minetti stood behind the counter, flipping pancakes like a man who had been doing it since birth. His mustached face split into a grin when he saw Lily and I walk in. He handed off his spatula and approached the counter.

"Well, well, if it isn't my favorite girl and her nosey friend."

Lily rolled her eyes as we hopped onto a couple counter stools. "Juli's got some questions about Liza Blake." She leaned forward and Vinnie kissed her cheek. They had been dating since I returned to town, and they really made a great couple.

Vinnie glanced at the bubbling griddle behind him before wiping his hands on his apron and focusing his full attention on us. The tension in his features hinted at the direction the conversation was about to take. His grin faded as he wiped his hands on a towel. "That woman? Trouble from the day she was old enough to know what she was doing."

I leaned my forearms on the counter. "Did she date one of your brothers?"

Vinnie sighed and gripped the edge of the counter. "Yeah. Tommy. Poor guy was head over heels for her. Thought she was the one. Then, out of nowhere, she drops him like a bad habit."

"Why?" I asked.

"This is where it gets good," Lily added, rubbing her hands together.

Vinnie scoffed. "Because she wanted Sierra Sweet's boyfriend. Just to prove she could take him. Liza had a way of setting her mind to something and making it happen—no matter who she hurt in the process."

Lily crossed her arms. "Sounds like classic Liza."

I exchanged a look with Lily, silently agreeing that this particular piece of Liza's past painted a sharper image of her manipulative streak. I hesitated before asking, "What do you know about a guy named Doug?"

Vinnie scratched his chin. "Now that's interesting. Doug was the one who got away."

I raised an eyebrow. "Got away?"

He nodded. "Doug and Liza dated for a while, but he wasn't blind to her bad side. He broke things off. Liza never got over it. Then Sierra turned around and started dating Doug just to stick it to her. That was one fight I wouldn't have wanted to be in the middle of."

I made a mental note to look deeper into this feud. "Do you think Sally Sweet would know more about it?"

Vinnie smirked. "Sally knows everything about everyone. If there's more to this story, she's your best bet." He pointed his finger at me and winked at Lily. "I'll make you girls the usual. Kyle will bring it out shortly."

"How's he working out?" I asked, knowing if Scott taught him, he'd be a super star.

"Eh, he's okay. He's no Scottie Iverson."

"Oh, no. Sorry about that, he seemed so eager."

I'm teasing. He's doing great. Free food is a definite motivator for that kid."

We all laughed. "Thanks for the information, Vinnie." Vinnie headed back to the kitchen. Lily and I sat in a comfortable silence.

Kyle soon appeared carrying a tray loaded with plates of strawberry crepes, two coffees and a small pitcher of cream. "Your breakfast is served," he said brightly, setting them down with a flourish.

The sound of laughter faded as my mind began working through the growing web of connections. Liza, Doug, Sierra—each name felt heavier with importance, and I knew I was closing in on the truth behind Liza's murder.

———

THE SWEET AROMA OF VANILLA, CARAMEL, AND FRESH-baked sweets greeted me as I stepped into *Sally's Sweet Treats*. The pastel-colored bakery was as charming as ever, with neatly arranged glass cases displaying an array of cookies, cupcakes, and decadent truffles. The tiled floor gleamed beneath the soft light of a crystal chandelier, while shelves of colorful jars filled with candy lined the walls, inviting you to indulge. The faint hum of the oven accompanied the soft jingling of the bell above the door, signaling my arrival.

Sally Sweet stood behind the counter, carefully arranging a tray of pecan turtles. She looked up and beamed when she saw me. "Well, if it isn't Juli Butler! What can I do for you, sweetheart?"

I smiled, stepping up to the counter. "I was hoping to ask you a few questions. It's about Doug."

Sally's hands stilled, her expression shifting. "Doug? As in Doug and Sierra?"

I nodded, eager to relay the tidbit of research I'd found within Liza's journal. "I heard a rumor they're engaged."

Her face softened. "Oh, yes! They're getting married soon. I was just about to put their engagement announcement in the paper."

I stepped closer to the display case. "Did Liza ever try to get him back?"

Sally sighed. "Liza never treated him well, and when Doug finally wised up and left, she hated that he never looked back. But Sierra? She and Doug are the real deal. He fell hard for her, and there was no turning back."

I leaned slightly against the counter, pretending to admire the tray of white chocolate coconut truffles displayed nearby. "Do you think Liza reached out to Sierra after things ended with Doug?"

Sally tilted her head thoughtfully. "Not directly, no. But she was bitter about Sierra's relationship with Doug. That much I can tell you. Even when she didn't confront either of them outright, you could see it in the way she carried herself for months afterward. Liza wasn't someone who let things go easily."

I nodded, absorbing her words. Liza's bitterness wasn't surprising, but it added another layer to her obsession with control, and her inability to deal with rejection. As I processed the information, something shiny caught my attention. The buttons on Sally's apron. My breath hitched. They looked familiar, identical to the button I had found off the trail.

Before I could ask about them, I noticed something else. On the back counter, near a collection of freshly sprinkled cupcakes, sat several spools of ribbon. One, in particular, made my pulse quicken. Lilac purple lace ribbon.

The same ribbon I had found in Liza's journal.

"That ribbon," I said, my voice steady despite the flutter in my chest. "Is it for a special order?"

Sally looked over her shoulder and chuckled. "Oh, that? No, I keep it around for gift-wrapping all my orders. Adds a special touch, don't you think? That shade is one of my favorites."

I smiled, nodding as I reached into my pocket, fingers brushing against the button I had found. I needed to think. To piece this all together before I jumped to conclusions.

"It is," I said casually, keeping my tone light even as my mind raced. "Liza ever buy any of your ribbons?"

Sally frowned slightly, her brows knitting together as she thought. "She wasn't much of a ribbon person. She liked things bold and flashy—not delicate like that. Come to think of it, I don't think she was in my store but maybe only once or twice."

Her answer threw me off, but I didn't let it show. There had to be a connection, even if it wasn't clear yet.

"Speaking of treats," I said, my eyes drawn to the display case once more, "I'll take a box of those sea salt caramels. You know, for investigative purposes."

Sally grinned. "Would that be for Chase?" She winked. "Or maybe Gary?"

I didn't hide my smile. "You know me too well."

She packed up the caramels and added a little something extra —a chocolate truffle for me. I handed her the cash and took the bag, my mind already working through the new pieces of the puzzle. As Sally handed over the bag, I hesitated.

"Sally, one more thing—Doug and Sierra's engagement...did Liza say anything about it?"

Sally's eyes darkened slightly. "Not directly to me, but she wasn't happy about it. When I saw her last, she came into *Nailed It!* salon just as I was sharing the engagement news with Betty and Sandy. Liza made a snide comment about Sierra 'winning again.' as she made her way to the pedicure station. It seemed petty at the time, but looking back...well, maybe it was more than that."

Her words clung to me like static as I left the bakery. The rhythm of my footsteps on the sidewalk matched the pounding in my chest. I knew one thing for certain. Doug wasn't just another name in Liza's past—he was a turning point. And if Liza had been holding onto that memory, there was a good chance it was tied to the reason she was murdered.

The ribbon. The button. Liza's bitterness toward Doug and Sierra—it all felt like scattered whispers of a secret refusing to surface. And in the middle of it all was Liza's journal, holding all the secrets no one wanted to acknowledge.

And now? I had a button, a ribbon, and a gut feeling that I was about to shake something loose in this case. But one thing was clear: Chase needed to know everything I'd just discovered. There was no time to waste.

Nineteen

The sheriff's station smelled of stale air and printer ink, the fluorescent lights casting a stark glow across the room. Chase sat behind his desk, flipping through a file with the kind of boredom that only came from routine paperwork. His uniform shirt was slightly rumpled, and his usual five o'clock shadow hinted that he hadn't had time for a proper shave. He looked up as I entered his office, brow furrowed in what I could only assume was a mix of surprise and suspicion.

I didn't wait for an invitation. I plopped the box of caramels onto his desk with a self-satisfied smirk. "I come bearing gifts and breaking cases wide open."

Chase sat straighter in his chair, his palms pressed flat on his desk. "What could you possibly have uncovered so early this morning?"

I pulled up a chair and slid closer, lowering my voice. "You seriously underestimate my ability to get people to talk."

He arched a brow but didn't say anything. Instead, he popped open the box, grabbed a caramel, and gestured for me to continue. "Bribery," he said with a mouth full of caramel. "Always effective."

"I went for a jog with Lily," I began, watching as he chewed thoughtfully. "We ended our run at *Ringo's*, where I got to talk to Vinnie."

"About what?" Chase eyed me curiously while blindly reaching for another caramel.

"He told me Liza used to date his brother, Tommy, but she dumped him because she wanted to prove she could steal Sierra Sweet's boyfriend. Apparently, this has always been a Liza's thing —taking what she wanted, no matter the cost."

Chase frowned, reaching for another caramel. "That's cold. But it doesn't scream murder motive."

I leaned in. "That's where things get interesting. Sierra's boyfriend was Liza's ex! Doug had dumped her and never looked back."

That got his attention. He sat forward. "Doug?"

"Yup. The same Doug she wrote about in her journal."

"Wait a minute, what journal? Juli, what did you do?"

"Why do you assume I did something?" I sat back and crossed my arms.

"Because you usually do." He took a sip of coffee from the black mug on his desk. "I'm on pins and needles as to why you have this journal, and it hasn't been turned in as evidence."

"I found it, thanks to Major and Scallywag. You don't need the play-by-play details."

"No." Chase leaned his chair back and crossed his ankles across the corner of his desk.

"Anyway, I shared what I found with Gary, and we've been working through some of the clues within the pages."

"Oh." He straightened with his feet back on the floor. "It still needs to be logged. He should know better."

"Well, I'm glad he hasn't taken it because I've been able to digest everything and find a new clue which has led me to the information about Sierra Sweet and her fiancé, Doug."

"Refresh me on this Doug character again?"

"Doug is Liza's ex. The one she never got over because he was the only guy who ever dumped her."

Chase gave a quiet hum of bemusement. "Messy."

I nodded. "And guess who can probably tell us even more about their feud?" I paused for effect and then added, "Sally Sweet."

At that, his skepticism returned. "Juli—"

"No, listen," I interrupted, digging into my pocket. "While I was at Sally's shop, I noticed the buttons on her apron matched one I found on the trail past Misty's booth, not too far from where Liza died." I held up a plastic baggie containing the small, round brass button, watching his expression shift. "I found it when Lily and I were jogging. I always carry a baggie for my cell phone in case it rains, so I tucked the button in it for safe keeping. I didn't really know the significance of it until I saw Sally's apron."

He took the baggie, rolling the button between his fingers. The doubt in his eyes wavered as they narrowed in my direction. "Great job bagging the button."

"Wait, there's more," I pushed, needing to build my case. "Sally also had spools of purple ribbon behind the counter—the same kind that was in Liza's journal. That's two solid connections."

Chase ran a hand through his hair. "It's circumstantial, but it's something. Enough for a conversation."

That was Chase's way of saying you might be on to something, but I won't admit it yet.

At that moment, the door to the station swung open, and Gary strolled in, carrying his usual air of easy confidence. His gaze landed on me and Chase, still hunched over the button. His lips quirked. "Well, well. What's going on here? You two sharing an investigative moment?"

I straightened. "I might have just given Chase his next big lead."

Gary raised a brow at Chase, who sighed and tossed the button onto his desk. "We need to pay a visit to Sally Sweet."

Juli stood. "Not without me."

Chase opened his mouth—probably to argue—but Gary clapped him on the back. "Come on, partner. You know she's not letting this one go."

Chase sighed, already resigned. "Fine. But if you touch or say anything you're not supposed to, I'm throwing you in the holding cell."

I grinned. "I'll take my chances."

———

COLEMAN'S PUB WAS THE KIND OF PLACE THAT FELT older than time itself. The wooden floors were worn, the walls decorated with faded autographed photographs of athletes who had passed through town, and the air was thick with the scent of beer and fried food. A low hum of conversation filled the room, punctuated by the occasional clink of a glass or burst of laughter from the bar. I spotted Oliver in the back, already nursing a pint. He had the kind of tired look that told me he'd been deep in thought—or trouble. Maybe even both.

I slid into the booth across from him. "You look like you could use a refill."

Oliver grinned, running a hand through his dark hair. "And you look like you just got away with something."

I shrugged. "I'll tell you mine if you tell me yours."

Before he could respond, a shadow fell over our table.

Rolf.

His figure was impossible to ignore, broad shoulders blocking out the light from the neon sign above the bar. His piercing blue eyes locked onto Oliver with an intensity that made my stomach tighten.

Oliver tensed but didn't look surprised. "Rolf. To what do we owe the pleasure?"

Rolf's voice was low, measured. "I'm done waiting, Oliver. You know what I want."

Oliver leaned back, casual on the surface but stiff beneath it. "And I told you, it's not that simple."

Rolf's gaze flicked to me, then back to Oliver. "Then let me make it simple for you. You have twenty-four hours to hand over the statue. No more games."

I frowned. "And if he doesn't?"

Rolf smiled, but there was nothing pleasant about it. "Then I make sure you both regret it."

A cold chill settled deep in my bones. This wasn't a simple debt collection. This was something far more dangerous.

Oliver clenched his jaw. "You're making a mistake."

Rolf didn't blink. "No, you made the mistake when you thought you could keep it for yourself and that my boss would never come looking for it." With that, he turned and disappeared into the crowded pub.

I released my breath in a giant whoosh. "Well. That wasn't ominous at all."

Oliver rubbed a hand over his face. "We're running out of time."

I narrowed my eyes. "Oliver, what is this thing really? Because Rolf isn't just some goon looking to make a quick buck."

He hesitated. "I'm assuming the statue is valuable."

"No kidding," I deadpanned. "But why? What's so special about this particular whale statue?"

Oliver hesitated, then sighed. "I don't know. I just know if Rolf wants it this bad, then there've got to be others who want it, too."

That was enough for me. If I wanted real answers, I needed to go straight to the source. There was only one person I could think of that would possibly have a clue as to who Rolf was connected to. I reached for my phone.

Oliver frowned. "What are you doing?"

I met his gaze. "I'm texting David."

His expression darkened. "Your ex, David? You really want to open that door?"

I swallowed hard. No, I didn't. David von Hoffster was the last person I wanted to deal with. But if he had information on Rolf—on the statue—I needed to know.

———

THE LATE EVENING AIR IN NEW HOPE WAS STILL AND unseasonably warm as I made my way home. David had returned my text, confirming he was free to talk whenever I wanted. Once inside my house, I curled up on the loveseat in my living room, knees drawn to my chest, a blanket tangled around me even though I didn't really need it. I held my breath and pressed the call button. The line rang. Once. Twice.

David answered after the second ring. His voice was smooth and smug, as if he'd been expecting me all along. "Well, well. Julianna, darling, to what do I owe the pleasure? Trouble in paradise with the good sheriff already?"

I rolled my eyes, even though he couldn't see it. "Still charming, I see. How's Rita? And the gallery?" Rita and I had kept in touch since she left her salon in New Hope to return to Boston with David.

There was a pause, as if he was caught off guard by the pleasantries. "Rita's fine. The gallery's chaotic, as usual. We've got a show opening next weekend—nothing stolen, nothing smuggled... yet." I let the silence stretch just long enough for him to feel it. "So why are you really calling?" he asked, amusement seeping into his tone.

"Trust me, you're my last resort."

David chuckled. "Always so dramatic. What is it this time?"

"Oliver also took something from the gallery as his final paycheck. A whale statue. I guess it's valuable enough that someone named Rolf Müller was sent here to New Hope to get it back." The line went quiet. I imagined David sitting in his sleek Boston office, probably leaning back in one of those ridiculous leather chairs he always insisted were 'vintage but comfortable.'

David whistled. "Ah. That statue. I wondered where it disappeared to."

I sat up straighter. "You know what I'm talking about? Tell me what makes it so important?"

David's voice dropped into something colder. "The statue's carved from a type of obsidian mined from a now-defunct island quarry. Only a handful exist. But this one...it's rumored to have a compartment. And whatever's inside? Let's just say certain people are willing to pay more than either of us could imagine in order to get their hands on it."

"Do you know what's inside it?" I asked, wondering what we'd gotten ourselves into.

"No idea. And honestly, I don't want to know. That's why I washed my hands of the whole thing."

I leaned my head back against the couch. "You were involved with Rolf?"

"He's bad news, Julianna. Don't mess with him. Give him the damn statue, and please don't add your usual detective antics."

"Antics? Really, David?" I kicked the blanket to the floor, as my annoying ex made my blood pressure rise.

"You know...all the crazy involvement you have when you think someone is in trouble."

"You mean help them? Because you can bet I'm going to help Oliver get out of this mess. Tell me what you know about Rolf Müller."

"Remember Matthew LeCreau?" David practically crooned, fully ignoring my outburst.

"Yes? Didn't he own—" I stood as the lightbulb went off in my head.

"Luxe Vista Grand Hotels," we both said in unison.

"What does your old buddy Matthew have to do with this?" I walked to my kitchen and poured a glass of wine.

"Let's just say that I'm hoping Matthew isn't involved but hey, you never know. I will tell you that he 'hosts' some questionable people at his various hotels from time to time."

"Questionable how?" I probed, needing more.

David was quiet again. "You need help?"

"No." The answer came out faster than I intended. But I meant it. "I get it. There's more you're not telling me."

"The less you know, the better darling. Take what I said to heart and just give Rolf what he wants. From what little I know, these are bad people, and they don't care about you or the other residents of New Hope. Do you understand?"

"How do you know all of this?"

"Because after you left Boston, I was offered in on a business venture by Matthew and I declined before I knew too much, if you know what I mean."

"Okay," I said softly, suddenly realizing Oliver and I had bitten off more than we could handle.

"Be careful. And Julianna?"

"What?"

"Just remember, if Rolf's involved, it means someone else is watching, too. He's never the only one."

I hung up, a sickening unease curling in my stomach like smoke.

I was beginning to understand Chase's issue with my Boston past. Nothing good had come from me working there. Nothing except Oliver, Amelia, and Nando. The best friends I'd do anything for, without question. While I waited for Oliver to return from Claire's, I decided some baking therapy was in order.

By the time Oliver arrived at my place, I was pulling the last batch of coconut chocolate chip cookies from the oven. I filled him in quickly—David, the statue, Rolf's interest in it. He paced while I talked, the floorboards creaking beneath his boots.

"We can't keep it here," he said, grabbing a cooled cookie from the wire rack.

"I know."

He glanced out the window as if expecting Rolf to be lurking in the bushes. "We've got, what, maybe a day before he shows up again?"

"Maybe less."

Oliver turned back to me, his dark eyes serious. "We need to stash it somewhere no one would think to look."

"Don't say my café."

He let out a quiet chuckle despite himself. "I wasn't. This time."

We both fell quiet, the magnitude of the situation finally settling in.

"Ollie, go get the statue. David mentioned a hidden compartment. Maybe if we can find it, and what's inside, we'll know why they are so desperate to get it back."

"Are you sure we want to do that? The less we know, the better, right? Didn't David say that, too?"

"Now is not the time to chicken out." My worry meter hummed to life over the imminent danger we were in. David's warnings seemed to be on repeat in my head. "Hurry up, we don't have much time," I ordered, catching the quiver of worry in my voice as I pointed toward the stairs.

Oliver bolted and returned wearing a fearful expression that mirrored my own. He placed the statue on the counter as if it were a bomb about to explode. "So, where do we look?"

I stared at the blue whale, rising from a turquoise wave, its fins outstretched and body leaning as if coming off a breach. "The base would be too obvious. Maybe one of these fins?" I touched each one thinking maybe they were a lever that would open the secret compartment. "Nothing," I grumbled. "What do you think?" I raised my eyes to Oliver, who had stepped closer to inspect the statue.

"Good idea, Jules." He wrinkled his nose in thought and ran his fingers around the circular base, up along the curled waves. "Wait, what's this here?" He picked up the statue, bringing it closer to both of our faces.

"What did you find?"

"This wave, right here closest to his belly. See that little line, a slight gap?"

"Yes," I replied, mesmerized, as Oliver placed his thumb on the cap of the wave and moved it forward. We immediately heard a 'click', and the bottom of the statue opened up. "Oliver, you found it!"

"So much for the bottom being obvious, huh?" he chuckled and lifted the statue so we could see what was underneath.

"It's empty," I sighed, my disappointment as heavy and the doom swirling in my gut.

"What do we do now?" Oliver closed the base and set it back on the counter.

"We do what David said and give Rolf the statue. We need to be ready for anything."

Oliver nodded, his jaw tight. "Then we've got work to do tonight. And fast."

"I'll handle Chase," I said. "He needs to know what's going on. Just...not the whole story. Not yet."

Twenty

The next morning, a heavy fog blanketed New Hope like a damp quilt. It curled around streetlamps and softened the edges of buildings, turning everything into a watercolor. My breath came out in little white puffs as I jogged beside Lily, the steady rhythm of our footfalls the only sound in the quiet morning.

"I'll never get tired of fog like this," Lily said, her breath even. "Makes the whole town feel like it's hiding something."

I gave a short laugh. "Maybe it is."

She glanced at me out of the corner of her eye. "You're talking about Liza again, aren't you?"

"How can I not?" I admitted. "There are so many valid threads. It seems like one pull in any direction could unravel the entire mystery." We turned down Main Street, the faded outline of *Petite Four Paws Café* barely visible through the mist. It looked like something out of a dream, familiar and a little eerie.

"I went over Liza's journal again last night," I said, dodging a puddle. "It's chaotic—rants, scribbled ideas, half-thought-out threats. Then there's one page. It's different. Focused. Almost like she'd finally figured something out."

"Let me guess. The page with the missing name?" Lily asked.

I nodded. "Yeah. Right under this line where she wrote 'final leverage.' But there's an indentation, like someone used the eraser end of a pencil, trying to wipe it clean. I can't make out what it says."

"Sounds like she didn't want that name found out."

"Exactly. It's bugging me. I've got everything else mapped out —the fight with Misty, the threats to go public, the *Sunflower Inn* stuff—but this missing name? It feels like the last piece of our unsolvable puzzle."

As we reached the café, the motion light clicked on with a soft buzz. The familiar scent of rain-soaked earth mixed with last night's baking prep, made my chest tighten in that way it always did when I entered my business. When I first decided to turn Mom's antique shop into a café for people and their pets, I didn't know if she would have been happy with my choices. But since making the space my own, while blending the old with the new, I didn't have a single doubt. This would have been a place she'd love to come to.

"Well, mystery aside," Lily said, performing a couple stretches as I unlocked the door, "I promised I'd check on your other dramatic case." We stepped inside and she added, "Where is the little rascal?"

Inside, the café was dim and quiet, chairs still stacked on tables from the night before, and the hum of the fridge filling the silence. The second the door clicked shut behind us, I called, "C'mon out Steve! Your favorite vet's here!"

Right on cue, Steve sauntered from behind the counter, favoring his front left paw like he was auditioning for a feline soap opera. Who knew what he'd been picking up from Scallywag and Major. For some reason, all the animals in my life had a case of drama llama syndrome. Steve blinked slowly at Lily, then looked at me like, *Finally, someone competent.*

"Oh boy," Lily said, kneeling. "What happened to you, baby?"

"He's been limping for a couple of days. I checked for splinters, swelling, thorns—nothing. But he's milking it for all it's worth. You should see all my customers who coddle him and buy him treats."

"Oh, you are a smart one, aren't you?" Lily scooped him up with practiced ease and carried him to the counter. Steve flopped onto his side with a dramatic sigh. "Front left?" she asked, already examining the paw. She pressed gently, working her way up to the shoulder and manipulated his joints while Steve did his best to look pitiful.

"No broken bones, no heat," she murmured. "And no wounds. Mobility seems to be fine. I'm guessing soft tissue strain. Probably jumped off something too high."

I winced. "Like the top of the cookie display?"

"Or every surface in here." Lily scratched his head as his tiny motor revved up. "Let's get you some medicine to help with any lingering inflammation."

She reached into her belt bag and pulled out a small amber bottle. Along with it came a tiny flashlight attached to her keys—sleek, metallic, and definitely not just for decoration.

I raised an eyebrow. "What's that?"

"This?" She held it up proudly, and I nodded. "UV light. Handy little thing. In my business, you never know when you'll need it—helps spot ringworm, pet stains, even certain bacteria."

I blinked. My mind returned to Gary's offhand comment at my house about how light can reveal what the naked eye can't—indentations, residue, erased words.

"Lily," I said, my voice catching with sudden excitement, "that might be exactly what I need."

Her eyes lit with curiosity. "What are we going to do?"

I was already halfway to my office. "Come on—I'll show you."

The office was still a mess of receipts, paperwork, and a growing list of customers' special orders. I pulled Liza's journal from my tote and flipped to the page I'd stared at a dozen times.

I pointed to the faint indentation. "See? You can almost make out something there."

Lily clicked on the UV light and held it low over the paper, angling it gently. At first, there was nothing. Then, as she tilted it slightly more—

"There," I breathed. "Wait—yes, right there!" Faint, but visible in slightly darker ridges, was a name.

Sally.

We stared at it, not moving, like it might disappear if we blinked.

"Sally?" Lily whispered.

"Could it be..." My brain flipped to the only Sally I knew. Circumstantial evidence, Sally. What if this was the proof we needed?

"Sally must have somehow known about Liza's journal. Maybe she erased her own name?" Lily said quietly.

I stared at the glowing name under the UV light. "Maybe she had a lot more to lose than we thought." Steve meowed from the doorway, as if to remind us of his continued presence—and importance. I turned to Lily. "Thank you for helping Steve, but you've also helped me gain more insight on this investigation."

She shrugged, running her hand along Steve's back when he jumped onto my desk. "Hey, just another day of helping animals and catching killers."

Steve pranced across my desk to gather more love, limp mysteriously forgotten.

I pulled my coat tighter as Chase, Gary, and I walked down the sidewalk toward *Sally's Sweet Treats*, the chill of autumn cutting through the crisp afternoon air. The bell above the door chiming with its usual cheerful ding. Sally was behind the counter, piping buttercream onto a tray of cupcakes. Her smile was instant and true to her name. "Juli! Sheriff! Officer Maxwell! What a wonderful surprise. What brings you all in?"

Chase gave a polite nod. "Just a few questions, Sally. About Liza Blake."

Sally's hands stilled. The frosting bag sagged slightly in her grip. "Liza? Not sure how I can help you there."

Gary leaned casually against the counter. "We're trying to get a clearer picture of her last few days. You two had some history, right?"

Sally gave a too-bright laugh. "Oh, years ago. Nothing worth gossiping about now. She was...complicated. My Sierra was her best friend until Liza became competitive with everything she touched."

"As seen by how she treated poor Misty," I muttered louder than intended, garnering a stern glare from Chase. I flashed a weak smile then busied myself by glancing around the shop. The familiar shelves of pastel-packaged candies and ribbon-wrapped boxes sat in neat rows. But something stood out. Sally's apron was different. New. Crisp. No frayed edges, no mismatched buttons. "You got a new apron?" I asked.

Sally blinked. "Hmm? Oh, yes. Just yesterday. Needed something fresh for the fall rush."

I exchanged a look with Chase, then pulled the bagged button from my pocket. "We found this. Near where Liza died. Matches the ones on your old apron, doesn't it?"

Her face paled. "Lots of people use those buttons. Could be anyone's." She giggled nervously, "I think we all did the same sewing project with our daughters when they were in junior high school."

Chase stepped up, his tone calm but firm. "We also found a purple ribbon. Like the one you use to wrap your boxes."

"Sheriff," her voice quivered. "I'm not sure what you're suggesting, but I have all kinds of ribbons that I use depending on the season."

"The lilac lace ribbon was found inside Liza's journal," I said as I stepped confidently next to Chase.

"I'm not suggesting anything," Chase continued. "I just have some questions to ask you."

"If you fully cooperate, ma'am, you have nothing to worry about," Gary added in that sweet voice he used to make people feel comfortable.

That did it. Sally's eyes darted toward the back door.

"Sally—" Chase started to speak, but she bolted. He cursed under his breath and followed, but I was faster. I leapt over a stool and pushed through the swinging kitchen door just in time to see Sally racing out the rear exit.

I burst into the alley, only to have Sally knock into me and try to dodge to my right. I managed to stay on my feet and grabbed the top of a trash can. Chase and Gary rounded the corner from the sidewalk, blocking her exit. Just as she pivoted, I let loose the lid like a frisbee. It wasn't the best shot, but it hit her behind the legs, knocking her to the ground.

I stood over her, catching my breath. "You want to explain why you're running from a simple question about buttons and ribbons?"

She glared at me, defeated. "You don't know what she was really like. None of you do."

Chase knelt beside her, handcuffs ready. "Then start talking."

And for the first time, Sally didn't have anything sweet to say.

After Chase cuffed her and Gary radioed for a cruiser, Sally sat slumped on a stool in the kitchen, her frosting-streaked shoes still dusted with flour. I stayed back a few feet, arms crossed, my heart pounding harder than it had during my wild runs across town chasing Major and Scallywag.

"I didn't mean to do it," Sally said, voice trembling.

"Then what did you mean to do?" Chase asked, calm but clearly unimpressed.

Sally looked up, eyes brimming with something between guilt

and exhaustion. "I only meant to scare her. That's all. Just scare her into leaving Misty and Sierra alone. She ruined people for sport. I couldn't take it anymore."

"Liza was a manipulator," I said, voice softening against my better judgment. "But murder, Sally? That's a league even Liza didn't dabble in."

"She ruined my daughter's career," Sally snapped, fire returning to her voice. "You want a motive? There it is. Sierra finally found someone—someone good in Doug Benson. And Liza couldn't stand it. She lost him forever because she was such a horrible person. She hated that she couldn't get him back, so she ruined Sierra's business career by twisting stories, sending texts under Sierra's name, posting fake information on social media, until the company she worked for let her go. My girl was devastated, but Doug stuck by her. He encouraged her to put herself back out there, and when the job came up on the west coast, he agreed to quit his job and move with her. Now they are engaged and so happy." Sally sniffed and then her eyes turned cold. "When that witch told me Sierra would be running home with her tail between her legs, I knew she was up to no good. She said Sierra should have known she'd never amount to anything and stealing Doug from her was the worst thing she could have ever done. Liza said she would make her life hell. I wasn't going to let that happen."

Gary lowered his notebook. "So, what happened that day?"

Sally placed her hands at the small of her back and stretched. "I brought her a gift basket. All sweet things. Candied apples. Caramel fudge. I made it look like a peace offering. I even tied it with the lilac ribbon Liza always mocked. She was in the middle of one of her tirades about Misty's baking and how she planned to call the health board on the *Sunflower Inn*. I lost it. I had a feeling Liza would terrorize poor Misty. I overheard her mention to someone how her cobbler had beat out Misty's several times. So, I took a chance. I had the bottle in my purse—I swear I only meant to give her a stomachache.”

“The poison?” Chase pressed.

“It’s not some mystery drug,” Sally said defensively. “It’s an old syrup—apple seed extract, concentrated. My grandmother used it to keep deer out of the orchard. Just a few drops are enough to turn your stomach inside out.”

“But you used more than a few drops,” I said.

“I was only placing a few on the cobbler when you showed up to talk to Misty. I got nervous and it came out too fast. But I didn’t think she’d eat the whole thing!” Sally groaned. “It was meant to be a warning. Something to make her rethink being so awful.”

I let out a long breath, the pieces clicking into place. “Liza had written your name in her journal. Probably planned to expose you in some public, humiliating way.”

Sally blinked, stunned. “She knew?”

I nodded. “She had written your name down but erased it. We were able to uncover it with a UV light. I think she realized she’d made a huge mistake by telling you so much about her hatred for your daughter.”

Gary stepped forward, flipping through his notes. “She had detailed entries on everyone she’d tangled with. But your name was the only one she erased. She may have been planning something against you, or strictly, your daughter, but we’ll never know. You eliminated her as a threat.”

Chase’s jaw tensed. “You’d better get a lawyer.”

“Already called for backup,” Gary said, motioning toward the siren in the distance.

My voice caught with both the severity of justice and the tangle of emotions that someone I’d known since childhood had turned out to be something darker. “How cruel. Your knowledge of sweet treats and old family remedies made you a killer.”

Sally looked down at her frosting-stained fingers like they

belonged to someone else. "I used to think sweet things solved everything," she whispered. "Turns out, they can ruin a life too."

By the time Deputy Caldwell and another cruiser arrived, Sally was silent. She didn't struggle, didn't speak, just nodded when they read her rights. Chase gave her a look that hovered somewhere between disappointment and resolve, and Gary followed them out with his notebook and that solemn walk he used when the case was wrapped but the feeling wasn't.

I stayed behind for a moment in the kitchen, staring at the tray of cupcakes she'd left behind. Perfect swirls of buttercream. Delicate sugar leaves. Sweetness masking something rotten.

Chase reentered quietly. "You okay?"

I nodded, not really sure I meant it. "Just thinking about how it all started. A ribbon. A journal no one could read."

"And a woman who thought vengeance could be baked into a cobbler."

I managed a tight smile. "We got her."

"Yeah," he said. "We did."

Twenty-One

The wooden floors of the *New Hope Historical Society* creaked under my boots as Gary and I stepped inside. Dust hung in shafts of morning light, catching on the edges of aged book spines and yellowing maps that curled in their glass cases like sleepy snakes. The smell reminded me of Mom's antique shop when I used to work there—wood polish, and whispers of the past.

The main reading room was empty except for the ticking of a grandfather clock and the occasional flutter of wings from the rafters. According to Mrs. Bailey, Scallywag had found a new perch up there last week. And despite her insistence that he was "only visiting," I had the distinct impression the parrot considered himself the guardian of New Hope's secrets.

"Mrs. Bailey's on her way," I said to Gary as I set my purse on the polished oak table near the far wall. "Apparently, she found the original deed and a few notes from the town committee that confirm the inn's historical protection status."

Gary pulled out the chair beside mine and sat. "That's a relief. Misty's going to lose it—but in a good way."

I smiled and sat across from him. "She deserves a win after the week she's had."

He looked at me for a moment, not speaking, and something in the quiet made my heartbeat change tempo. It was that sudden awareness, when you realize you're no longer just talking.

"So," he said, his voice low, "you want to tell me how it felt chasing Sally Sweet through a bakery kitchen? Because that has to be one for the books."

I laughed, the sound easing something inside me. "Messy. Smelled like a vanilla victory. She would have made it out of the back alley, if you and Chase hadn't gotten there when you did."

Gary leaned back in his chair, palms splayed on the worn wooden table. "Awesome use of a trash can. Very resourceful."

"Thank you very much," I said, grinning.

His eyes softened, and the roguish glint gave way to something quieter. "And how are you—you good?"

The question caught me off guard. Not because it was unexpected, but because it came from a place I hadn't fully let myself feel from Gary before. Genuine care. Concern. Maybe something else.

"I'm...okay," I said. "It's been a long few days."

"Chase hasn't really checked in with you since Sally's arrest, has he?" The way Gary asked wasn't accusatory. Just careful. Observant. But it hit harder than I expected.

I shook my head slightly. "Not really. He's been buried in paperwork and coordinating with the mayor's office. Which makes sense. That's his job."

Gary nodded but didn't press. I could see it in his eyes—he wanted to say more. Maybe ask if I wanted something different from Chase. Maybe offer something more himself. But instead, he sat back in the chair and let the silence stretch out again.

We just sat there for a second, looking at each other. Not talking. The kind of silence that didn't need filling. It wasn't long before the back door creaked open, and in swept Mrs. Bailey in her usual swirl of vintage floral print, cat-eye glasses hanging around her neck, and an old metal ring full of antique keys.

"Well now," she announced brightly. "If it isn't New Hope's finest mystery solvers. Are we ready to put some rumors to rest?"

I stood, grateful for the momentary escape from my tangled thoughts. "We are. You found the deed?"

"Right here," she said, setting a thick folder between us. She opened it with a ceremonious air. "The *Sunflower Inn* is officially listed under the 1932 Historical Preservation Amendment. That means the town board cannot approve any renovations or demolitions without a full vote and environmental review. And given how beloved that inn is, there's no way any such vote would pass."

Gary leaned in. "Which means Victor Langley's claim on needing to 'rescue' it with vacation rentals is invalid."

Mrs. Bailey nodded. "Exactly. Misty trying to run the inn was never a threat to the inn's legacy. The inn was protected all along. She just didn't know about the funding we had to handle any repairs, or the limitations tied to the property. Now she'll have the paperwork to prove it."

I let out an easy breath. "Thank you, Mrs. B. Misty's going to cry when she hears this."

"She'd better." Mrs. Bailey sniffed, dabbing at her eyes anyway. "I always thought her parents gave her all the information on the inn before they retired and left town. I guess it slipped their minds."

"Maybe they did, and she just forgot?" I said, feeling uncomfortable by Mrs. Bailey's distress. "And she's always had Ethan to help with things."

"Well," Mrs. Bailey continued, "Misty has worked harder than anyone I know to keep that place running. And I say that as someone who once helped paint the ballroom ceiling during a summer thunderstorm by candlelight."

We all laughed, and as the morning light brightened the windows, I knew things were finally beginning to fall into place.

But even as the relief settled in, a knot of uncertainty twisted in my chest.

"Juli?" Gary's voice was soft, and it pulled me back.

I blinked him into focus. "Hmm?"

"Hey, you kinda zoned out for a second there."

I glanced at Mrs. Bailey, who had busied herself by flipping through old survey maps near the back wall, giving us privacy. "Yeah. Just...thinking."

"About Chase?"

The directness of it made my breath hitch. But I nodded. "It's not that he doesn't care. I know he does. But sometimes I think I finally..." I swallowed to gather the courage to say what had been on my mind for days.

Gary's brows pulled together, concern written in the tight line of his jaw. "You deserve someone who shows up for you, even when it's uncomfortable and not ideal."

I looked down at my hands. "He does. He has. But I keep wondering if maybe I've expected too much. Or if I'm just afraid to admit that maybe...we weren't meant to last."

Gary didn't say anything right away. Instead, he reached across the table and covered my hand with his. Just a moment. Warm. Steady.

"You don't expect too much," he said, quietly. "You've been carrying so much on your own. Someone should be carrying some of it with you."

I felt my throat tighten, and I had to look away before the emotions got the better of me.

Mrs. Bailey returned with a stack of photocopies and laid them beside the deed. "Here are some of the committee notes, just in case Victor tries to twist things. This one even has a comment about how the inn's foundation uses stone from the original mill. That's historical gold right there."

Gary cleared his throat and scooched his chair back, giving me space, though the warmth of his gesture lingered. "That should seal it then."

"Between this and Sally's confession, I'd say we've done all right for one week," I said.

But even as I said it, I wasn't sure what I meant by "We." Chase and I started this investigation. But lately, it had been Gary beside me more often than not. He asked the right questions. Gave me space when I needed it, and presence when I didn't even know I did.

And now, I couldn't ignore it anymore—that quiet shift. The way his eyes lingered just a second too long. The weight of that touch. The way my chest reacted, equal parts comfort and conflict.

Mrs. Bailey handed me the file with a smile. "You tell Misty she has a whole town behind her. And not just me and my crusty archive folders."

I gave her a warm hug. "Thank you, for all of this, really."

As she stepped into the hallway to grab tea, Gary and I stood in the stillness.

"You don't have to say anything," he said, his voice almost a whisper. "I just needed you to know...I see you, and I'm not going anywhere. That's all."

I didn't know what to say. I wasn't ready. But I didn't pull away either.

Scallywag squawked from above us, breaking the moment. "She knows! SHE KNOWS!"

I let out a laugh that sounded more like a choked breath. "I swear, that bird is psychic."

Gary smiled. "Or maybe he just picks up on what the rest of us haven't said yet."

And as I gathered the papers and we walked out into the crisp afternoon, I realized that maybe—just maybe—it wasn't only the case that had changed. Maybe I had, too.

———

I walked into the *Sunflower Inn* later that afternoon. The foyer gleamed, the hardwood freshly polished, autumn wreaths adorning every doorframe. Misty had even replaced the vases with fresh mums—orange and yellow and rust red.

Oliver stood near the fireplace, his hands in his pockets, admiring some of Misty's family photos she shared on the mantle. He turned with a half-smile as I entered.

"Well?" he asked.

I held up the folder. "The inn is safe. Mrs. Bailey found the original documents. It's protected. Misty's cleared."

Relief flooded his face. "Thank God."

A sharp squeal echoed from the hallway, and Misty rushed in, cheeks pink and eyes already glistening. "The mayor just called! Juli —oh my gosh!" She threw her arms around me, nearly toppling us both.

I laughed and steadied her. "You're officially cleared. And no one's taking the inn away."

Behind her, Ethan appeared, slower, more reserved. His suit jacket was wrinkled, his tie askew, but the look in his eyes was focused and clear.

"Misty," he said, his voice shaking a little. "Can I—can I say something before this day gets any more perfect?"

She turned toward him, surprised. "Of course."

He stepped closer, holding her hands. "I messed up. Not because I didn't love you—but because I let my parents talk me into thinking that legacy was more important than our future. They didn't mean to hurt you. They just didn't know you like I do. They didn't understand how deeply you care about this place. But I do."

Tears slipped down Misty's cheeks. "Ethan—"

"I love you," he said. "And I'm so sorry I didn't stand up to them sooner. I should've. I'm asking you to forgive me. And I'm asking you...to marry me."

A stunned silence followed. Misty blinked, let out a watery laugh, then cupped his face in both hands.

"Of course I forgive you," she whispered. "I totally understand. I should have seen how strong you were...how strong we are together. I'm sorry I didn't."

They kissed, and the room filled with the sound of everyone clapping—the cook from the kitchen, Gary from the doorway, even Mrs. Bailey, who must've snuck in while I wasn't looking.

I watched them—Misty and Ethan—so tangled in joy and forgiveness that it pulled at something in my own chest. I felt a familiar ache and couldn't help but think of Chase. Of all the times I'd pushed him away, not sure I could let someone in that far again. Yet, he always stood by. I wasn't sure how his presence in my life was going to exist anymore. What if I'd really pushed too far this time?

Oliver stood beside me, silent.

I glanced over and caught him watching them, too, but the look on his face wasn't heartbreak. It was clarity.

"Ollie, you okay?" I asked.

He nodded slowly. "Yeah. Actually...yeah. Watching them just now—I think I finally get it. Misty was never really mine to hold on to. And I'm okay with that."

I saw it then—the shift in his posture, the lightness that hadn't been there before. "You gonna tell Claire?"

He smiled, a real one full of promise and hope. "The first chance I get."

"Good," I said, nudging his arm. "I'm happy for you."

He laughed, and we stood there together, both of us freer than we'd been that morning, as the sun gleamed through the stained-glass windows of the *Sunflower Inn*. The light caught the edges of the glass and spilled across the polished floor in long stripes— amber, rose, and violet stretching like ribbons through the foyer. It bathed Misty and Ethan in a glow that felt too cinematic to be real, as if the universe had decided they deserved their ending. Maybe they did. Maybe this was how stories sometimes wrapped up in real life.

Oliver and I lingered in the soft hush that followed. Even Gary had quietly stepped back, giving them space, leaving the moment to settle like dust. My gaze drifted back to the whale statue perched on the mantle. Oliver had angled it like it belonged there, nestled among the antique candlesticks and family photos—a sleek, blue-gray sculpture carved from some rare stone that had made us targets in Boston.

"You sure that's the best hiding spot?" I asked quietly.

Oliver glanced at it, shrugged. "It's hiding in plain sight. No one would expect me to be that bold. And besides,"—he flicked his eyes toward the front door—"Rolf's not dumb, but he's not exactly subtle either. If he shows up here, I'll know."

I raised an eyebrow. "That's a pretty big gamble, Ollie."

"I know." He rubbed a hand along the back of his neck. "But I'm done running. I've done enough of that for one lifetime. You and me both."

I didn't respond. Not out loud. But a part of me curled tight inside at the thought—that maybe some of us were still running, even if our legs weren't moving.

Misty laughed again, the sound light and a little breathless as she wiped the corners of her eyes. She turned to me, her voice thick with emotion. "Thank you, Juli. You saved me. You saved the inn."

I gave her a tight smile, something twisting behind my ribs. "You saved yourself, Misty. You just needed someone to hand you the proof." I paused a moment, wondering if now was the right time. "Can I ask you a question?"

"Of course, you can ask me anything."

"Why did you get a loan at the bank if you weren't using it for the inn's repairs."

"Wow, small town gossip." She glanced at Ethan and then back at me. "My brother needed help with some medical bills for his wife. Mom and Dad aren't in a position to help him like they used to, so I took out a loan against the inn. All of a sudden, things started happening here and I couldn't keep up when reservations began to decline."

"That won't be an issue, now," Ethan said, his expression softer, more grounded as he slid an arm around her waist. But Misty's body tensed slightly at the gesture, and her eyes darted to me.

"I'm still mad at you, Ethan," she said, the declaration coming out with a stubborn kind of fire before turning to me. "Don't let the proposal fool you."

Ethan didn't flinch. "I know."

Misty stepped out of his hold and faced him squarely. "I can forgive a lot. But I still can't believe you let your parents manipulate things like that. That you even considered letting them force us together like some business deal. You're lucky I even listened."

Ethan's face reddened, but he didn't drop his gaze. "I didn't just consider it. I agreed to it at first."

The silence after that was sharp and electric.

"I told myself it was the right move," he went on. "That maybe love would come later. But then it did come. Not because of what they wanted—but despite it. When you turned down my proposal the first time, I was crushed. And weirdly relieved. Because I realized I didn't want you because marrying you would save the inn. I wanted you because—because you're Misty. You're this whirlwind of color and warmth and loyalty. You make everything feel like home."

Misty's jaw trembled, but she kept her arms folded.

"I didn't know how to tell you that without sounding like I was just trying again for all the wrong reasons," he said. "But I love you. I've loved you for a long time now. And I'll wait as long as it takes for you to trust that."

The words hung between them like an echo. Even the creak of the old floorboards seemed to pause. Oliver inhaled softly beside me, almost like he was absorbing the confession himself. When I glanced over, his eyes were shiny, but not with pain.

He turned to me, his voice low. "He's her Ethan."

I nodded slowly. "Yeah. And Claire's yours."

We stood in the fading light, watching Misty stare at Ethan like she was seeing him for the first time. Maybe she was.

Oliver murmured, "You think everyone gets one?"

I didn't answer right away. My heart thudded against the memory of Chase's voice. His hand on my wrist. His name in my phone that I kept almost calling. The weight of what we hadn't said. What I hadn't let myself admit.

"Maybe," I whispered. "But not everyone gets to keep them."

Oliver looked over, curious. "You talking about Chase?"

I didn't deny it. "I don't know if he's my Ethan. I used to think he was. Before Boston. Before everything got tangled in the past. But now..." I trailed off, feeling the sting of unshed tears build behind my eyes. The sight of Misty and Ethan—bruised, flawed, whole—made something ache inside me that I couldn't quite name.

"I think love like that—real, stubborn, patient love forgives the things that matter and lets go of the things that don't," I said slowly. "But some wounds? They don't scar over as easily as you think they will."

Oliver nodded, like he understood that kind of damage. "It's scary, huh? Thinking you might never stop being afraid of getting hurt again."

I let out a shaky breath. "It's terrifying."

We stood like that for another long moment, letting the noise of the world ease back in—the kitchen's clatter, the creak of the stair rail, someone's quiet hum of an old folk song drifting down the hallway.

Then Misty broke the silence again.

"Juli?" she called, her eyes clearer now, her hand wrapped around Ethan's.

I looked up.

"I think I said yes," she said, her voice quivering with disbelief and giddiness. "I mean, I didn't technically say the words, but I kissed him and I'm not kicking him out, so…"

I laughed and crossed the room to pull her into another hug. "You said it loud and clear."

When I pulled back, Ethan extended a hand to me. "Thank you, too. For sticking around. For believing in her when she didn't believe in me."

I shook his hand, firm and steady. "Don't make me regret it."

He smiled. "I won't." As they turned toward the stairs—Misty giving him orders about fixing the guest book software before anything else—I let myself exhale fully.

The inn was safe. Misty was safe. And maybe, just maybe, I was on my way to being safe, too. Not from Rolf. Not from Boston's shadows.

But from the fear I'd been carrying since the day I left Chase in my rearview without a word. It wasn't a fix. Not yet. But it was a start.

And sometimes, that was enough.

Twenty-Two

I had walked into the sheriff's department with the intent of telling Chase I had contacted David. I figured I could handle the fallout if he got upset. After all, David was the only person I knew with access to Rolf's world, and we were out of options. The station always smelled faintly of coffee and copier toner, with the quiet hush of a place trying not to feel like tension lived in its walls. I'd been in it more times than I could count, but today my steps slowed just before I reached his office door.

I heard voices. Not the official, serious tones of law enforcement chatter. Softer. More personal. I paused without meaning to eavesdrop, my hand halfway to knocking.

"You've been grumpier than ever," April's voice said lightly, but there was something behind it. "I get it. You're frustrated, and I know you don't want to talk about it. But whatever's going on, you need to deal with the problem. I'll keep being here for you, but..."

There was a pause.

"You have to decide what you want, Chase."

I froze.

There was no response from him, at least none I heard. Just

183

silence. Then footsteps. I backed up instinctively and slipped into the hallway, ducking into the small records alcove across the hall just as April walked past, her head down.

She didn't see me.

A second later, I remembered to breathe and crossed to his door, knocking once before stepping in.

Chase looked up from his desk, his jaw tight. "Juli."

"Hey," I said carefully. I didn't bring up what I'd overheard. I wasn't even sure what it meant. Instead, I crossed my arms and cut right to it. "I called David."

He frowned. "von Hoffster."

I nodded. "I told him we needed information on Rolf. Anything. Even a whisper."

Chase stood, pacing once behind his desk. "You couldn't have told me first? What if David makes things worse? I don't trust him."

"It was a risk," I admitted, "but we're short on time and Rolf keeps circling. I trust David to keep his head. He still respects me, Chase."

He turned sharply toward me. "That's what I'm worried about."

There it was. The unspoken thing. Always simmering. I opened my mouth to respond but didn't get the chance. Gary walked in without knocking, as if he'd sensed the tension and decided to diffuse it with his usual confidence.

"Hey, Boss, Juli," he said, giving me a nod and a small smile. "Hope I'm not interrupting anything too serious."

"You are," Chase muttered.

"Perfect," Gary said with a grin, unaffected, and walked straight to me. "Just wanted to see if you'd like to walk the festival with me tomorrow? Since it's the last day, I thought we could grab some kettle corn, people-watch, maybe not talk about murder."

I blinked.

Bold move, right in front of Chase. But there was something in

Gary's gaze—not pushy, just steady. Like he was offering me a choice, not demanding one.

"That sounds great," I said, watching Chase from the corner of my eye. His expression didn't change, but the flicker of something —recognition, maybe—crossed his eyes. He nodded once at Gary, too polite to object.

Too proud to say anything more.

"Looking forward to it," Gary said to me, then turned back to Chase. "Boss."

And just like that, he was gone.

Chase stared at the door long after it clicked shut, his shoulders tight, his mouth set in a line that could cut glass.

I turned back to him, swallowing down the strange blend of adrenaline and awkwardness still lodged in my throat. "I'll let you know if anything David said turns up to be substantial," I said, realizing now was not the time to discuss the information my ex had given me. Based on what I'd heard from April, and now Gary's bombshell, Chase had plenty on his mind already. Plus, I couldn't take the chance he'd shut down what Oliver and I had in mind.

He gave a curt nod. "Be careful, Juli. Rolf's dangerous."

"I'm not afraid of him," I said, and sort of meant it.

"I'm not worried about you being afraid," he said, softer now. "I'm worried about what it's costing you not to be afraid when you should be."

His words settled in the space between us like dust, fine and weightless but impossible to ignore. He rubbed the back of his neck, looking suddenly exhausted. "This whole thing's been pushing you too far. And if something happens—"

"Nothing's going to happen," I cut in gently. "I'm being smart."

"You're being brave," he corrected. "And that's not the same thing."

I didn't respond. I just nodded and stepped out, the air

between us still thick with everything we couldn't seem to say. The story of our lives.

The sunlight outside was bright and sharp, casting shadows along the sidewalk that looked too long for mid-afternoon. I paused just beyond the front steps, letting the breeze cool my skin and trying to shake the lingering sense that I'd walked into the middle of three conversations and finished none of them.

April's words echoed faintly in my head.

You have to decide what you want, Chase.

I didn't know what that meant—if it had anything to do with me or nothing at all—but it rattled around inside me all the same. It was hard to untangle anything lately, least of all where I stood with the people who mattered.

But I wasn't walking away from this.

Oliver and I had a plan. It was a little messy, and undeniably dangerous—but it was better than standing still. It was action. And right now, I needed that more than clarity.

I checked my phone. A text from Oliver blinked on the screen.

I'm at the café. Where are you?

I smiled despite myself. Of course he was at the café. We were heading into the heart of something risky and unknown, and the man wanted caffeine. Typical Oliver.

With one last glance back at the station—at the window where I knew Chase sat behind his desk, probably still brooding—I turned and headed toward the café. There were questions waiting, and not all of them had to do with Rolf. The truth was, I didn't have time to untangle Chase's heart right now.

I had work to do.

———

THE WOODEN CHIMES SUNG THEIR INVITING TONES AS I walked into my café, where Oliver sat at our usual back table, nursing a cup of coffee that had probably gone cold. He slid a folded note across the table without a word. I sat and picked it up. The message was short and to the point.

Tonight. 9pm. Pepper's Motel. Bring the statue or someone gets hurt. No more chances.

I looked up. "So, this is it. We're really doing this?"

Oliver ran a hand through his hair. "Yeah. I'm really drawn to the statue. I thought I could handle keeping it as my own little secret. I never thought it would be part of something possibly illegal."

"Think about it, Ollie. David and the gallery were involved in a lot of bad things thanks to Eddie. More than one illegal thing was bound to happen. Your piece just happened to be the one."

"Even so, I thought I could stay one step ahead, you know? But it's not worth it anymore. Not if it means someone's life is threatened, or worse."

I leaned back, my heart heavy. I hadn't realized until this moment how much tension I'd been carrying. "Good," I said. "I mean, not good that we're still dealing with Rolf, but good that you're ready to be done."

He nodded, then gave me a curious look. "How did things go with Chase?"

I sighed, stirring the iced latte in front of me. "Complicated as usual. I overheard April telling him he needed to deal with 'the problem,' whatever that means. And then Gary showed up and made plans to see the last day of the festival with me right in front of him. Chase didn't say anything, but I could tell it landed."

Oliver wore a knowing look. "Gary's nothing if not direct."

"He's also patient," I said, almost to myself.

Oliver didn't comment, just watched me.

"Anyway," I continued, folding the note, "we should meet up at *Pepper's* around eight-thirty. Better to be early. I don't want Rolf getting antsy."

"Agreed."

We sat in silence for a moment, the low hum of the espresso machine behind us filling the air. Oliver tapped the table lightly. "After tonight, I'm done looking over my shoulder. I want a real life here in New Hope. With people who actually care."

I reached across the table and squeezed his hand. "Then let's make sure this ends tonight."

He turned his hand, lacing his fingers with mine briefly before letting go, his eyes focused. "I mean it, Jules. I've been living on edge since Boston. Always looking over my shoulder, never fully relaxing. New Hope feels different. You, Misty, Claire, even Chase in his grumbly, righteous way—it all feels...real."

I smiled at that. "Well, we do specialize in cozy chaos around here."

He gave a soft laugh, then sobered. "Rolf scares me, though. I won't pretend otherwise."

I nodded, my worry meter rising. "I know. That note wasn't just a bluff. He means it."

Oliver looked around the café. A few locals sat near the front, chatting over pastries. Fire Chief Frank was at the counter, waiting for his usual. Everything looked so normal. It made Rolf's threat feel even more jarring.

"I don't want this place to get caught in the crossfire," Oliver said quietly. "You've built something here, Jules. Something warm and good. I can't be the one who ruins that."

"Hey," I said, my voice firm but gentle. "You're not ruining anything. You're fixing it. You're standing up to him. That counts for something."

He cracked his knuckles, clearly not convinced, but didn't argue.

"What about Claire?" I asked. "Are you going to tell her about tonight?"

He shook his head. "If we come out of this clean, then I'll tell her everything. The whole truth. She deserves that."

"She does," I agreed. "So do you."

He looked at me, surprised. "Me?"

"Yeah," I said. "You deserve a fresh start, too. Not one buried under secrets and stolen sculptures, but a real one."

He sighed softly. "I want that more than anything."

The door chimed again, and Oliver and I startled. He glanced over his shoulder, and when he saw it was just Mark dropping off an invoice, he relaxed. But that split second of tension reminded us both what we were walking into tonight.

"We should talk through the plan," I said, lowering my voice. "You'll have the statue. I'll hang back and observe. If Rolf makes a move that feels wrong, I'll have Chase on speed dial."

Oliver hesitated. "You think he'd come?"

I thought of the look Chase gave me as I left his office. The warning in his eyes. The care he still hadn't quite managed to hide. "Yeah," I said finally, as the truth settled deep in my chest. "I know he would."

Ollie gave a slow nod. "Then it's good to have a backup. But let's try not to need it."

I smiled faintly. "That's the goal."

We sat in silence again, letting the importance of the evening ahead settle over us. This wasn't just about the statue anymore. It was about ending something that had been following both of us for far too long. The clock on the café wall ticked past four. Still hours to go until the meet, but it already felt like the countdown had started. The calm before the storm.

"You should go rest for a bit," I said, finishing my latte. "Take some time. I'll close up here and grab the statue from the inn. We'll meet at *Pepper's*, like we planned."

"You sure?"

"Positive."

He stood, pulling on his jacket. "Thanks, Jules. For not walking away from this."

I stood too, reaching out to lightly squeeze his arm. "Just promise me you'll be careful tonight. No heroic last stands, okay?"

He gave a tired but genuine smile. "That goes for you, too."

As he walked out, I watched him go with a mix of hope and dread. Tonight, everything could change. For better or worse, we were putting the past behind us—one way or another. I glanced at the folded note on the table, then tucked it into my pocket.

No more chances, Rolf had written.

And hopefully, after tonight, no more Rolf.

Twenty-Three

The gravel crunched beneath my tires as I pulled into the lot behind *Pepper's Motel*, headlights slicing through the dusk. I spotted Oliver crouched near the tree line, half-hidden in the bushes with a clear view of the picnic table by the woods. His posture was tense, eyes fixed on the clearing where we were supposed to meet Rolf.

I eased my truck into a spot near the side of the building and killed the engine. My hand was on the door handle when a familiar engine growl rolled into the lot behind me. I froze.

Gary.

He pulled up beside me, windows down, one arm resting casually on the steering wheel. "Hey," he said with a lazy grin. "Wasn't expecting to see you here."

Panic flared. I stretched my arm beside me and grabbed the first thing within reach—an old pastry box on the passenger seat—and stepped out, holding it like it contained secrets of the Lollipop Guild.

"Kitty Krackers," I blurted. "One of my regulars ordered them. They weren't ready earlier, and I promised I'd swing by on my way home."

Gary stepped out of his car and walked toward me, a suspicious squint to his eyes. "At *Pepper's Motel*?"

"I know," I said with a sheepish laugh. "She's staying here during the festival. Not everyone books early, you know. I figured she'd appreciate the effort."

He didn't look convinced. Not fully, anyway.

He stepped a little closer. "You don't have to make excuses, Juli. If this is about Chase..." I braced myself. "...he's a big boy. He can handle it. Whatever's going on between us doesn't need to tiptoe around his feelings."

This wasn't the time or place for a conversation I wasn't ready to have. I smiled tightly and pivoted.

"You're right. I just really need to get this to her and get home. Big day tomorrow—final day of the festival. The booth, the café prep...it's a lot."

He studied me for a beat, then nodded. "Looking forward to more time with you since we're not chasing suspects or dodging danger."

"Me, too," I said quickly, already stepping backward. "See you tomorrow, Gary."

He gave a short wave, climbed back into his car, and pulled away. The second he was gone, I tossed the box back into my truck, then grabbed the box containing the statue and darted into the brush where I crouched next to Oliver.

"Took you long enough," he murmured. "Everything okay?"

"Gary almost blew the whole thing," I whispered. "Let's do this."

We approached the picnic table together, cautious but steady. The woods beyond were quiet, the only sound the soft hum of insects and the occasional rustle of wind through the trees.

Rolf stepped out from the shadows.

He wasn't alone. Two men flanked him—both taller, broader, and definitely packing weapons. Rolf, as always, looked amused.

"Charming," he said. "I expected just Oliver. But you're always full of surprises, Julianna Butler."

"We brought the statue," I said evenly. "We're not here to make trouble."

"No, you're just here to tie up loose ends." He narrowed his eyes, a faint glint of something sinister flickering behind them. "You've seen too much. You know what I look like." He paused for emphasis. "That's a real problem in my world."

Oliver shifted beside me. "You said this was just a drop. No threats. No games."

Rolf's grin curled with dark amusement. His voice dropped to a chilling whisper, "I lied."

I stepped forward, my voice clear. "If anything happens to me, David will know. And believe me, he doesn't play nice."

Rolf chuckled. "David and his Boston goons? Please. The people I work for don't scare that easily, and frankly, neither do I."

"You might not be scared of David," I said coolly, even though the rush of blood pounded in my ears, "but I know who your bosses hide behind. David has connections—real ones. Global ones. You sure you want to test that?"

Rolf's jaw clenched, his eyes burning with cold fury. His voice cut through the air like a blade, "Enough talk. Hand over the statue."

Oliver boldly moved forward, holding out the box containing the statue. "What's so important you'd kill over it? What are you hiding?"

Anticipation and greed gleamed in Rolf's eyes. "Everything that matters. Power. Leverage. And enough dirt to make kings bow."

The air grew still. Then a voice rang out from within the trees.

———

"I KNOW EXACTLY WHAT'S IN THE STATUE," CHASE SAID, stepping into the clearing, gun drawn and steady. "An encrypted data drive containing names, dates, financial records—everything the Bellemonte Cartel has kept buried."

Rolf flinched, then pulled me in front of him like a human shield. "You're bluffing."

"Try me," Chase said coldly.

"Watch yourself, sheriff, or I'll put a bullet in her."

I pinched my eyes shut as I felt cold steel against the back of my head. I wondered if Chase knew the compartment was empty, like maybe someone had gotten to it before Oliver took the statue.

Chase commanded Rolf's attention. "You were sloppy. And now it's over."

A crack of brush signaled someone else arriving.

"Not exactly alone either," said Rip, the town coroner, stepping from farther down the tree line, shotgun in hand. Walt Harris followed behind him, a baseball bat slung over one shoulder.

"Thought you might need a little backup," Walt said casually.

Gary appeared at Chase's side, his gun pointed toward the henchmen. "Surprise."

Rolf snarled, ordering, "Take them."

His men started forward—but chaos erupted before they got far.

A shriek split the air as Scallywag dive-bombed the first thug, talons flashing. The man yelped and swatted wildly, stumbling. A low growl followed, then a blur of white and black fur barreled into the second man. Teeth bared, full throttle.

Major.

"What the—" the man didn't have a chance to finish.

Deputy Liam came running through the trees, out of breath. "They broke out of the station—bird and dog. Scallywag was screaming your name, Juli. Major tore down the door. I followed 'em here in the cruiser."

Rolf pushed me to the ground and turned to run. Major

launched. Gunfire cracked. I screamed, ducking as Chase grabbed me, shielding me with his body. When I looked again, Rolf was on the ground, howling. Major had him pinned, jaw locked on his forearm. Gary and Liam had the two henchmen cuffed and disarmed. Chase never let go of me as he stepped forward, tossing his cuffs to Gary.

"Hold him down," he said. "Major—off."

The dog hesitated, then backed off, still growling. Rolf writhed in pain, his face contorted.

I turned to Chase, adrenaline still pulsing through me. "You, you followed me?"

He gave me a look. "When you didn't answer my message, I knew you were up to something."

I tried to come up with a sassy retort, but all I could manage was, "You weren't supposed to be involved in this."

He blinked, then surprised me with a slight grin. "Too late for that. When my deputy reports something suspicious that may or may not be happening, I tend to listen. Besides, you should know by now, keeping you safe is worth breaking every rule in my book."

My thoughts raced, his words lodging themselves in the cracks I thought I'd carefully sealed. Keeping me safe. Even now, after everything, he still cared. A pang of something sharp and familiar flared in my chest—hope, or maybe regret. I wasn't sure which scared me more.

Behind us, Liam slapped cuffs on Rolf with a grimace. "That's gotta hurt. Gonna be an interesting cause of injury to write up."

Walt tossed the bat over his shoulder and surveyed the scene. "You kids have the most interesting evening plans." He shook his head as he walked away.

"So, tell me, how did you know about the encrypted drive?" I turned back toward Chase. "Ollie and I found the secret compartment, but it was empty." I wrung my hands, contemplating my next question. "Is Oliver still in danger?"

"Jason, my FBI contact, told me the whale's eyes were the

trigger to open the back fin. The micro drive has been safely delivered. Both Oliver, and you, are out of danger."

"Thank you," I said and stepped into a hug.

"Anyone up for a celebration at *Coleman's*?" Gary muttered, brushing dust from his jacket and I separated from Chase.

"Count me in! Mind if I ride along?" Oliver eagerly replied and rushed to catch up with Gary.

"What about you?" I asked weakly, wondering where Chase's mind was at.

"I've got to help Liam get everyone logged in and settled, make some calls." He chuckled and motioned toward Gary and Oliver. "Keep them in line until I get there."

"Roger that," I said with a quick salute before I jogged toward my truck.

And just like that, it was over.

For now.

The ballroom of the *Sunflower Inn* hadn't seen this kind of crowd in decades. It had been polished to near perfection, the chandeliers glittering like stardust overhead, casting flickers of warmth across the glossy wood floors. A band played soft jazz near the back, just beneath the grand arched windows, and for a moment, it almost felt like we'd time warped—somewhere around 1937, when glamour was effortless and evenings like this were something to dress up for.

Mrs. Bailey had pulled out the original linen tablecloths she claimed were hand-stitched by the inn's founder. Trays of finger foods were carried around the room. Tiny cucumber sandwiches, bacon-wrapped figs, and mini cranberry scones—courtesy of Oliver and Claire— were arranged in artful spirals on silver platters. He'd pulled from one of his catering menus and tweaked it with an old-time flair.

The whole town had turned out. Mayor Montgomery stood at the center of it all. She was mid-speech, hands gesturing grandly as she addressed the crowd from the small stage that had once hosted swing bands and wedding quartets.

"...and I think we can all agree," she said with a wide smile, "that this year's Fall Festival was one for the books. Despite the tragedy we faced, it was the hard work of Sheriff Hargrave and his team who not only found justice for Liza Blake but also captured a man who's been on the FBI's Most Wanted list for over two years."

The crowd erupted in applause. Chase, standing near the back of the room, gave a modest nod. He was in his uniform, though the tie was a little loose, the sleeves slightly rolled. I watched him from my spot near the fireplace, my glass of champagne growing warm in my hand.

"And," Mayor Montgomery continued, "let's not forget the woman of the hour—Misty Shepard. Through setback after setback, Misty kept the *Sunflower Inn* afloat, showed incredible grace under pressure, and still managed to serve the best dessert table this side of Hartford."

More cheers and a couple shrill whistles echoed through the ballroom. Misty, standing beside the mayor in a deep burgundy dress that matched the fall blooms on the tables, blushed and waved. When the oversized check for the revitalization grant was brought out, she looked like she might cry. I knew what this meant to her. To the inn. To the town.

I slipped through the crowd once the applause died down and found my way to Chase. He was near the punch table, his hand resting on the back of a chair, like he wasn't sure if he should stay or head for the exit.

"Hey," I said softly.

He turned. His smile was the tired kind—genuine but worn around the edges.

"Hey, yourself," he said, then added, "You clean up okay," as his eyes took in my green wrap dress and tall black boots.

"And you look downright heroic," I replied with a smile.

He laughed lightly. "Don't tell Rip. He and Walt are still running on adrenaline. They're already insisting on a commemorative plaque."

"I mean it, Chase. Thank you. For stepping in with Rolf."

His smile faded just a touch. "You shouldn't have been there."

"I know. But I was." I paused and looked up from beneath my lashes. "And I'm glad you were, too."

For a moment, the room fell away. We stood in a quiet pocket of air and noise, neither of us saying the things that might shift the glossy planks beneath our feet. His eyes lingered on mine, then flicked down toward the floor, like he might say something more.

Then Gary appeared. "Well, well," he said, sidling in with a broad grin and a glass of Betty's spiked punch. "If it isn't New Hope's Nancy Drew and her noble backup."

Chase stiffened beside me. "Real funny."

Gary extended his glass in a toast. "Seriously, Juli. Your investigating gave us half the momentum we needed to wrap this up. The sheriff here should be giving you a badge."

"She does enough dangerous stuff without the badge," Chase said.

Gary chuckled. "All I'm saying is—without her? We'd still be wondering why a parrot was screaming bloody murder in the trees."

I tried to laugh, but Chase had already stepped back.

"I need to check in with the mayor." He nodded to both of us. "Good work, Julianna."

And then he was gone, weaving through the crowd with a steady stride, disappearing toward the back door. Gary didn't seem to notice, or didn't care.

"I know I've said it before," Gary continued, "but I meant every word. I'm not just here for a good time or to watch you save the day. I want to be here—for you. If that's something you want, too."

I opened my mouth, unsure how to respond. Thankfully, I didn't have to just yet.

Lily came bounding toward us, her wavy hair bouncing, Vinnie trailing behind her in a much more measured fashion. "Juli!" she called. "I've been looking all over for you!"

"She can't stop talking about all of your clues, and the journal. Said she couldn't tell me anything until the case was solved," Vinnie said, smiling. "She wants to be your mystery-solving sidekick."

Lily nodded. "Every hero needs a sidekick, right?"

"Of course!" I laughed. "You're welcome on any case, any time."

Lily beamed. "I can't wait to help out!"

"Shhh, that has to stay on the down-low." I placed my hand on her shoulder to contain her energy I loved so much. "You have to remember, sometimes I insert myself before being asked to help."

Gary leaned in. "Let's hope there aren't more cases. One crime wave per season, right?"

I gave a noncommittal shrug, but my eyes scanned the crowd again, instinctively seeking out Chase. I found him near the hallway, leaning against the wall. He wasn't watching me—not directly—but he was holding his phone, scrolling with that focused, far-off look he got when something was bothering him. Then, as if he felt me staring, he looked up.

Our eyes locked across the room.

For one beat. Two.

Then he slipped the phone into his pocket, turned away, and walked into the lobby.

Gary was saying something beside me, but the words were muted. Mrs. Bailey waved from the dessert table, and I used it as my excuse.

"I think I'm walking home with Mrs. Bailey tonight," I said quickly. "She made those molasses cookies again. I owe her a taste test."

Gary looked disappointed but didn't argue. "Sure. Another time?"

"Maybe," I said, with a soft smile. He gave me a quick kiss on the cheek and stepped aside to go talk to Fire Chief Frank and Rip.

I walked toward the dessert table, past the band, past the celebration. Mrs. Bailey greeted me with a paper napkin and a warm cookie. But my eyes drifted once more toward the lobby doors—where Chase had gone.

Where the ghosts of our past lingered in the silence, and every unspoken word was a choice neither of us dared to make.

———

THE AIR OUTSIDE THE *SUNFLOWER INN* WAS COOLER than expected, the last breath of fall lingering in the wind as I walked side by side with Mrs. Bailey down Main Street. The festival lights still twinkled behind us, casting a golden glow over the town, but here in the quiet stretch between the inn and home, it was still. Peaceful.

Mrs. Bailey linked her arm with mine, her pace slow and steady. "You know," she said, "I've been thinking about the girl who sat on my porch months ago, talking about how she hoped her mother would approve of her choices."

I smiled fondly. "I remember that night."

"I do, too. You looked like you were trying to convince yourself more than me. That your mother wouldn't be disappointed. That you didn't still carry a torch for a certain brooding sheriff."

I chuckled. "Maybe I was in denial."

Mrs. Bailey squeezed my arm. "Maybe. But denial doesn't stand a chance when you grow into the kind of woman you're meant to be. And honey, you've grown. You're not the wild, reckless teenager who used to sneak into the woods after curfew. You're a woman who makes things happen. Who gets answers when no one else can. Your mother would be proud of you. Not just for what you did with Liza's case, but for the way you carry yourself now. Steady. Brave."

I swallowed the lump forming in my throat. "Sometimes I still feel like I'm winging it. I still take risks. If I hadn't, I never would've agreed to help Oliver."

"Sweetheart, taking risks isn't the problem. It's the kind of risks that matter and how reckless you are in taking them. And yours? They come from a good heart. You just get a little... misguided now and then."

"That's generous," I said on a laugh.

Mrs. Bailey grinned. "I'm known for it. But really, sometimes the heart is worth the risk. Even when it scares you."

I looked ahead to the warm porch lights glowing in the distance. "What if I can't?"

"You won't know if something is worth the risk...unless you take it."

We turned the corner, and the familiar sight of Mrs. Bailey's porch came into view. The rocking chair I had once sat in still creaked in the wind, just like it had that night months ago.

As we reached the steps, Mrs. Bailey paused and turned to me. "You worry too much. The heart's compass always finds its true north. And you don't even have to click your heels."

I laughed. "I'm glad one of us is confident."

She stepped onto the first stair, leaning on the railing. "Just remember, Juli-girl, sometimes your story doesn't end where you expect—it just turns the page."

"Goodnight, Mrs. B." I wrapped her in a hug, feeling a piece of my mom in her return squeeze.

"Night, love. Don't let your keys—"

I didn't hear the rest. I stepped off the sidewalk with a little too much bounce in my step and tripped on a crack in the pavement. The small ring of keys flew from my hand and skidded across the concrete, landing near a pair of worn boots.

Boots I knew all too well.

I looked up, and there was Chase. Holding Major's leash in one hand, my keys in the other.

"Well," he said, stepping forward, "you always could make a dramatic entrance."

Our hands met as he passed the keys back to me. His fingers brushed mine, warm and familiar. Neither of us pulled away.

"Walking Major?" I asked, my voice softer now.

"Yeah. He gets restless when he's got too much leftover energy at the end of the day."

"I get restless when there's too much left unsaid," I murmured before I could stop myself.

His brow lifted just slightly, his mouth tugging at one side in a way that told me he'd caught the weight of those words. "I was gonna stop by earlier," he said. "But then I figured...maybe you needed some time."

"I thought about stopping you at the inn," I admitted. "But then Gary showed up, and well..."

"Yeah... Well," he echoed. He looked down at Major, then back at me. "We've always had pretty bad timing, huh?"

"Infamously bad."

For a moment, neither of us said anything. The wind rustled through the leaves overhead, the sound of home settling around us like a favorite quilt. On the porch behind me, Mrs. Bailey cleared her throat. Loudly. "Don't mind me. Just checking the...porch railings."

We exchanged a quick glance, momentarily united in the quiet amusement of sweet Mrs. Bailey.

"I should get Major home," he said, finally breaking the moment.

"Yeah. And I should..." I motioned toward my house lamely. "Get inside before I fall over another sidewalk crack."

He smiled. "Night, Scarlett."

I stepped back, watching as he crossed to his own porch. His steps were slow, like he was waiting for something. Maybe even hoping.

I stood at the edge of my walkway, holding my keys tightly. "Hey, Chase?"

He turned back.

"Goodnight," I said. "And...thanks again."

His smile was faint but real. "Always."

I watched him disappear inside, then glanced up at Mrs. Bailey, still lingering on her porch, now pretending to untangle her wind chimes.

"You're really bad at pretending not to eavesdrop," I called up.

Mrs. Bailey grinned. "And you're really bad at pretending you don't care."

I looked down at my keys, then across the arborvitaes where Chase's porch light had just flicked off. Maybe she was right. Maybe the heart always did find its way home. I turned toward my own door, a bittersweet smile tugging at the corners of my mouth. There truly was no place like home.

And maybe, just maybe, my next chapter was going to be mine to write.

Also by Barbara Witek

A Juli Butler Mystery

Cracker Jacked

Sugar Snapped

Half Baked

About the Author

I live in upstate New York with my very own alpha-male who puts up with my crazy author tendencies and my even crazier imagination!

I'm a firm believer in love at first sight, second chances and creating your own destiny. Isn't that what romance is all about? Being a hopeless romantic helps me write my touching, emotional and heartfelt romances. I also love a good mystery and trying to figure out whodunnit, along with the feeling of being swept into another time through historicals.

When I'm not writing, I'm in love with life on 2 wheels! I've recently gone from being a passenger to driving my own motorcycle. The thrill never gets old and I love the rush of starting that engine and taking off. Every ride is an adventure and I see the open road and world around me so differently. And of course when I'm not cruising, I enjoy a good glass of wine-or whiskey-and getting lost in a book. I also love cross-country skiing and ice-skating (although I admit to not having done either in years!) hiking, anything crafty, and competitive family game nights (scrabble of course)! And dogs. I love them and want to adopt them all!

I love to connect with my readers, fans, and other authors. Come find me and let's chat it up! Here's how: